THE
NIGHT
RIDE

Also by J. Anderson Coats

The Green Children of Woolpit

R Is for Rebel

The Many Reflections of Miss Jane Deming

THE NIGHT RIDE

J. Anderson Coats

ATHENEUM BOOKS FOR YOUNG READERS

New York London Toronto Sydney New Delhi

A
atheneum

ATHENEUM BOOKS FOR YOUNG READERS
An imprint of Simon & Schuster Children's Publishing Division
1230 Avenue of the Americas, New York, New York 10020
This book is a work of fiction. Any references to historical events, real
people, or real places are used fictitiously. Other names, characters,
places, and events are products of the author's imagination, and any
resemblance to actual events or places or persons, living or dead, is
entirely coincidental.
For information about special discounts for bulk purchases,
please contact Simon & Schuster Special Sales at 1-866-506-1949
or business@simonandschuster.com.
The Simon & Schuster Speakers Bureau can bring authors to your
live event. For more information or to book an event, contact the
Simon & Schuster Speakers Bureau at 1-866-248-3049 or visit our
website at www.simonspeakers.com.
Interior design by Debra Sfetsios
The text for this book was set in Meridien LT Std.
Manufactured in the United States of America
0921 FFG
First Edition
2 4 6 8 10 9 7 5 3 1
Library of Congress Cataloging-in-Publication Data
Names: Coats, J. Anderson (Jillian Anderson), author.
Title: The Night Ride / J. Anderson Coats.
Description: First edition. | New York : Atheneum Books for Young
Readers, [2021] | Audience: Ages 8 to 12. | Summary: Saving her coppers
to buy a beloved horse that has been transferred to the royal stables of the
king of Mael Dunn, new stablehand Sonnia must compete in a dangerous,
highly illegal Night Ride to protect her horse.
Identifiers: LCCN 2020046452 | ISBN 9781534480773 (hardcover) |
ISBN 9781534480797 (ebook)
Subjects: CYAC: Horses—Fiction.
Classification: LCC PZ7.1.C62 Ni 2021 | DDC [Fic]—dc23
LC record available at https://lccn.loc.gov/2020046452

*To everyone,
young and old,
who dreams in
hoofbeats*

1

IT'S BEEN YEARS since I was small enough to ride Buttermilk, but she's still the best pony in this whole town.

Buttermilk is who you lead out when a kid isn't sure he wants a pony ride. She is round and soft with big, dark eyes under a shaggy white forelock, her back so broad it's like a nice, sturdy chair. Her step is so even that kids forget they were scared and start pretending they're rangers, or bandit hunters, or fleet riders.

When the ride is over, kids hug her goodbye. Sometimes mothers have to drag them by the hand off the town common while they bawl and plead for another turn.

Hazy likes to kick up her heels. You put an adventurous kid on her back, or one who's a little older, or who's ridden before. Boris is strong enough to carry two kids at once and sweet enough to be willing to do it. I love all three of our ponies, but Buttermilk is the one that keeps bringing in kids.

This is why she's the best pony in Mael Dunn. It's definitely not her attitude. She breaks wind like a dock-hand and enjoys nabbing hats off passersby. She'll eat apples and candy sticks right out of the hands of children who aren't paying attention to their treats.

But every time I put a kid on Hazy or Boris or Butter-milk and lead them in a well-trodden circle on the common, we earn a copper piece.

More kids mean more coppers, which means every pony ride puts me a little closer to making Ricochet my own.

Greta and I are supposed to trade off every other day, one of us giving pony rides and the other going to school, but Father found out she was letting me have her turns on the common because she'd rather go to school and I'd rather be with the ponies. We both got in trouble, and there were extra chores and a lecture about honesty, but that's when Father started giving us one copper out of every twenty that each of us earned from rides.

My sister puts her coppers aside to buy books.

I'm saving for Ricochet.

Mother and Father can only afford the half-day school session, so the instant that noon creeps near and Mistress Crumb reaches for the handbell on her desk, I'm already gathering my copybook and pencil stub.

Before the ringing stops, I'm out the schoolroom door and galloping through the lanes. I duck into our house just long enough to dump my copybook and change into trousers, then it's a quick canter to the royal stables where they spread out like a crescent hugging the steep mound topped by the castle.

There's an armed guard at the entrance, of course. A ranger who drew the short straw. They're used to me, though, and I'm always waved inside with a bored flick of the hand.

To my right is where the royal family's personal mounts are housed. I've never been through that door, but I like picturing the king's beautiful stallion and his daughters' ponies content in giant box stalls.

Straight ahead are the cavalry horses: big standard-breds that are all muscle and Arabians that can run forever. If a soldier's going to ride it, it lives down that straight-ahead hallway.

But I turn left, into the long corridor lined with stalls where the fleet horses live.

They're not called *fleet* simply because of their speed. These are the working horses of the royal household. If a message must be sent to a neighboring kingdom, the courier gets a mount here. If one of the princesses needs a coach-and-six, these are the stalls they'll clip-clop out of.

These horses are a fleet, like a fleet of ships.

I'm counting. Sixteen stalls down. Face left. And

there he is. Shining chestnut coat. Beautiful brown eyes. Four white stockings up to his knees.

Ricochet.

I let myself into his stall and press my face against his neck. He smells clean, like someone just rubbed his coat with fresh straw.

So far I own roughly one of his hooves. I did the figuring on a day when Greta and I were cleaning pony stalls out behind our house. Ricochet is worth fifty gold dinars. There are one hundred coppers in a dinar. So to buy him, I will need five hundred coppers.

Right now I have twenty-two coppers. I keep them in a small linen bag that I drew a horseshoe on with berry ink.

We scrubbed walls and floors that day and tried to decide how to divide Ricochet into parts so I'd know when I earned what part.

"I don't think it matters," I tried to tell her. "Master Harold says I can't have him until I can pay all fifty dinars."

"No, it does," Greta assured me. "You'll need to earn a lot of coppers, and there's going to be a point when you get discouraged. You'll want to spend all your money on candy sticks just to have something *now*. But this way, you can tell yourself: Look, I already own one hoof. Twenty more coppers and I'll own *two*. Buying Ricochet will seem possible, and when something seems possible, it's that much easier to make it happen."

Greta is pretty smart for someone who's only ten. I'd say it was all the school, but she was this way long before either of us started going.

I kneel and put a hand over Ricochet's left front hoof and whisper, "I won't let you down."

There's an echo of bootsteps, and I leap to my feet in time to see the royal stablemaster rounding the corner. Master Harold is big like a draft horse, with the same powerful, deliberate strides and shaggy mane. He waves, then makes his way down the aisle toward me.

I've known Master Harold since I was tiny. He's laughed at our hearth and eaten at our table and shared more than one mug of cider with Father. But he goes home to a four-story townhouse with real glass panes in the windows and eats meat at every meal, and when he stops outside the stall, I curtsy with the ends of my shirt.

"Time for our ride," I say, patting Ricochet's neck, and even though Master Harold has told me hundreds of times that I don't have to ask permission if Ricochet is in the pasture or his stall, I add, "If that's all right."

"Yes. About that." Master Harold strokes his whiskery chin. "Ricochet is in top form largely because of you. All that time on the exercise course. The extra attention—grooming, bathing, fussing. And that's on top of his sweet, calming nature."

My heart goes still. "You're selling him."

"Sonnia." Master Harold puts a big hand on my shoulder in some version of a hug from an old man with no kids of his own. "It's not my choice what the king decides to do with his horses. But I meant it when I said I'd do what I could to keep Ricochet from being sold to anyone but you. Besides"—he's teasing now—"you're the only one who wants him."

I've known the rhyme since I was a little kid. *White on his forehead, white on his feet, grind up his bones and throw away the meat.* I don't say it aloud, though. I don't want to hurt Ricochet's feelings.

"Ricochet's been chosen to be a companion for the king's newest racehorse," Master Harold goes on. "Perihelion is supposed to tear up the track this season, but he's high-strung and skittish. He needs a good calm friend to walk beside him before the starting bell and settle him down."

Only Master Harold hasn't yet looked me in the eye. He's still blocking the door of Ricochet's stall.

I bite my lip and ask, "What does that mean?"

"Well . . . Ricochet will have to live at the racetrack all season. So he's not going to be here for you to fuss over till winter."

I study the ground. Pet Ricochet's nose again, once, twice, to keep the tears back. Of course he's been chosen to walk with a skittery racehorse. Ricochet is the best, most peaceful and happy gelding in this whole stable.

"Well." I lift my chin. "The track is pretty far, but I'll figure out a way to get over there to exercise him. It won't be every day, but—"

"There's a rider already chosen." Master Harold still isn't quite looking at me. "The boy's name is Paolo. He'll be riding Ricochet exclusively while he's there. Not really a job for a girl, is it? Even a horsey one like you."

Master Harold laughs uncomfortably, but my mouth falls open.

"I can't even ride him? I've been coming here every other day for more than three years and—"

"I beg your *pardon*!" snaps the royal stablemaster, and I startle and drop my eyes and curtsy again because I forgot for a moment who I am and who he is.

Master Harold shuffles awkwardly, and I can tell that he feels bad for raising his voice, but also that he doesn't. Still, his tone is careful and precise when he says, "Perihelion has all the makings of a champion. Ricochet can help him achieve that, and this decision is final. Approved by the king. Do you understand?"

I nod, then whisper, "Can I visit him there?"

"You can, but you should know Ricochet will have handlers and trainers who'll need him to be in certain places at certain times." Master Harold looks away. "You won't be able to just walk in like you can here."

Ricochet whuffles. He really is in top form. A silky coat that shines like a newly minted copper. Strong shoulders, graceful haunches. Smart, too.

I helped him get this way. It's like he's partly mine already.

Master Harold is in charge of the royal stables. I can

come and go here because he and Father have known each other a long time. I don't know what I'd do if I turned up one day and the guardsman on duty refused to let me in.

"I understand." I make myself smile. "I can still ride him today, right?"

"He was supposed to be at the track this morning," Master Harold replies gruffly. "I kept him here this long so you could say goodbye."

I stand close to Ricochet so he can put his nose on my shoulder. I'm going to miss his warm breath on my cheek as we say hello. I'm going to miss seeing the world from his back. I'm going to miss the way he'll wait till I'm not paying attention, then lick my whole face from chin to eyebrow, just like a dog.

"Paolo should be here soon to ride Ricochet over," Master Harold says as he walks away. "A stablehand will be along to get him ready to travel, so now's your chance to fuss over him."

I'm allowed to ride Ricochet on the exercise course anytime he's not on a fleet mission, but the stablehands are the only ones who can groom and feed him. They put on his saddle and bridle while I watch. I can't even adjust the stirrups.

It doesn't seem glamorous to be a stablehand, but everyone connected to the royal stables receives free room and board on top of a portion of the income from everything the horses do. The king gets twenty shares.

Master Harold gets twelve. Fleet riders get three and grooms get one. Stablehands get a quarter share.

Master Harold may be in charge of the royal stables, but the king loves horses and personally approves every man or boy who so much as lifts a shovel here.

They don't come from the lanes, either. They come from families who have been taking care of royal horses for generations.

All but Torsten. My brother has a position here because Master Harold has no kids of his own and his years of service have earned him a single big ask.

"Sonnia, hey!"

Torsten appears in the aisle, grinning and holding a lead rope. The royal stables are huge, and even though I'm here a lot, we don't always run into each other. Sometimes it's because he's so busy, but other times I avoid him on purpose.

I'm supposed to be happy for my brother. The royal stables offer an incredible opportunity for an unremarkable boy from the lanes of Mael Dunn. It's a future that can be counted on, one that will let him escape the hand-to-mouth scrabbling for hiring fair contracts that last just a year, that everyone in the lanes must take to make a living.

I'd be happier for him if such a thing were possible for girls.

Torsten asks how Mother and Father and Greta are doing, and I fill him in as he leads Ricochet out of his stall. The faint shadow of the moustache he's so proud of looks less like a smudge of dirt than it did last time, and when I tell him so, he musses my hair till I shove his hands away, giggling like we did when he lived at home.

The stable aisle opens into the sprawling paddock full of horses being curried and having their hooves picked. It's sunny, and there's a nice breeze that blows the fresh green smell of the pastures beyond. Nearby, a sturdy bay mare is standing saddled while a fleet rider checks his message bag.

At some point growing up, every kid in Mael Dunn wants to be a fleet rider. You hear about brave couriers rushing urgent trade agreements to neighboring kingdoms and outriding bandits and arriving just in time with medicine or vital news. Then you learn they mostly do boring things like deliver invitations to royal cotillions.

I can't think of anything better than spending whole days in the saddle, just you and your horse. Whatever the message.

A boy I don't recognize is leaning against the tack shed. His gray riding jacket and breeches look new, but he's rangy like a quarter horse and his brown wrists stick out well beyond the cuffs. He's smiling as if he's among old friends.

I know pretty much everyone at the royal stables, so he must be Paolo.

Master Harold said a rider had been chosen. He didn't say the rider would be a kid my age. If the rider was going to be a kid my age, there's no reason it couldn't be me.

Except for all the reasons it couldn't be me.

2

I AM BITING my lip. I am not going to cry.

Torsten is saddling Ricochet, but it's not the one I use to ride. This saddle is newer, and there's a purple cloth under it, and even though I know the color is meant to let Ricochet through all the tollbooths for free, it's not our old felt pad, and my stomach lurches.

Paolo crosses the paddock, nods politely at Torsten, then puts one shining boot into the stirrup.

Ricochet is leaving today. He'll be gone for months. I'd ride with a whole bandit company if it means spending another few minutes with him.

I slip back into the stable, hurry down the corridor, through the entryway, and along the side of the building until I come to the moss-damp gate where horses emerge into the city. I don't have long to wait. Soon I hear the distant clopping of hooves coming at a sedate walk, and Paolo and Ricochet appear at the top of the path.

Paolo gives a little half-wave as I approach. "Hey there. Didn't I see you in the paddock just then?"

I'm a little out of breath as I fall into step by his stirrup. "This is going to sound weird. But can I ride along with you? To the track?"

He peers at me, then makes a strange gesture, bringing both hands in front of him near his belly. I don't know what to make of it—until it hits me.

If Paolo's been chosen for Ricochet, he's from a riding family. The same people who become fleet riders and rangers and sometimes win a place in the cavalry. I've just asked to sit close behind him in my grubby thirdhand trousers and shirt stained with horse slobber. All the way through Mael Dunn. In front of everybody.

While I'm trying to work out how to explain, to apologize, Paolo smiles in a friendly way and holds out a hand. "Trying to avoid the road tolls? Can't blame you for that."

"Thank you." I try not to sound relieved as I settle onto Ricochet's rump behind the saddle. I hold on with my legs and let my arms dangle, deliberately not touching Paolo's fancy jacket.

If I close my eyes, I can pretend it's just me and Ricochet.

"You picked a good day to visit the track," Paolo says. "Deirdre's riding Perihelion in the breezing runs. It's almost the same as a race, but you don't have to pay to see it."

As if I have coppers to spend on admission to the racetrack.

"Basically, the horses gallop four furlongs at not-quite-racing speed," he goes on, "and those times are how the betting office decides on odds for the pay table, so it's still pretty exciting."

"Deirdre," I echo, and just saying the name makes me smile. We used to have a babysitter called Deirdre. For nearly a year, before Torsten was old enough to be in charge, she would turn up when the sky was barely pink to look after us while Mother hurried out the door to get to the sweatshop before the whistle blew.

"She's hoping her times are good enough that the trainers will choose her to ride Perihelion in the next race," Paolo explains.

"I heard how a girl won a spot among the king's jockeys a while back." I wait, but Paolo doesn't mutter something mean about how being a jockey is a man's job. So I add, "People keep saying she was raised by bandits. Do you think that's true?"

"I think bandit companies are a lot more complicated than people realize."

We're coming up on the city gate. The racetrack is just outside the walls. Paolo will expect me to climb down so he can take Ricochet to wherever Perihelion is, and I'm not ready to say goodbye.

"Do you know her?" I ask. "Deirdre? Do you think I could meet her?"

Paolo shifts enough to glance at me. His smile has faded. "You hoping to be the next girl jockey?"

I laugh aloud. I might as well hope to be adopted into the royal family. Not just anyone gets to be one of the king's jockeys. There's a tryout, and you have to turn up in proper racing silks and make one of the twelve fastest times of anyone there, including jockeys who already ride for the king.

Exercising a fleet horse every other day is a world away from knowing how to win a race.

Paolo faces forward in the saddle once more. The gate isn't far now. There's a grid of blue sky at the top where the iron portcullis has been raised for the day's comings and goings.

Somehow it's easier to talk to his back. "It's just . . . if one girl jockey rides racehorses for the king, that means there could be another someday. Then another, and another, and if there's enough of them, people might leave off the *girl* part and just call them jockeys."

As I talk, Paolo's shoulders relax. When he turns again, his grin is real. "You're in luck. I'm pretty sure Deirdre will be where we're going."

Soon we're passing through the southern gate. There are no houses or shops outside the walls here, just the racetrack sprawling into the open space all the way to the greenwood. There's a series of grandstands for town-house people and special viewing boxes for the nobility and royal family and any visiting dignitaries. The stables and outbuildings stand on the left-hand end of the oval, and beyond them lie ancient, dense forests that span as far as a horse can run in a week.

I shiver. I can't help it. There are bandits in the greenwood, but they don't stay long near the city walls. They drift through the forest, moving from place to place, stealing anything that's not nailed down—especially horses.

This forest all but overhangs the pastures. It must be full of rangers. Just in case.

It's not a race day, but the track is busy regardless. Horses are everywhere, and riders too, and stable grooms and trainers and the occasional owner in fancy brocade. They're boys and men, but I'm used to being the only girl not in riding clothes in places with lots of horses.

I can't look away from those horses. Bays, roans, grays, chestnuts. Shiny black horses and splashy pintos and horses scattered all over with tiny spots. Braided manes. Arched tails fluttering like banners.

It's like paradise.

Paolo gently directs Ricochet toward a series of long stable buildings facing one another across a wide dirt horseway. The buildings on the left spread out big and glorious like a nobleman's country estate. There are racehorses in the pastures attached to those stables.

I love Ricochet, but he is nowhere near the horse that any of them are. You can tell at a glance that those horses have been bred, trained, fed, and fussed over—vitamins, rubdowns, supplements, insulated blankets—so they'll look like this. So they'll perform like champions and win races and fat purses.

A pale gold stallion dances in front of the closest stable, surrounded by a dozen grooms and trainers. He's huge, easily seventeen hands, and so muscly that the jockey on his back looks like a little kid.

"That's Perihelion," Paolo says over his shoulder. "Let's get down."

I slide my legs over Ricochet's rump, but I'm barely on the ground when Perihelion grunts and rears, forelegs thrashing, and grooms and trainers leap out of his way. His rider shortens the reins and leans forward, and when the stallion comes down, he kicks and stomps at the dust.

Master Harold was right. Perihelion does need a calming influence, because he almost threw that poor jockey twenty feet into the hard dirt of the horseway.

Perihelion's rider swivels him in a circle, trying to calm him, singsonging, "Dang it, Helie, what is wrong with you lately?"

That voice.

All at once I'm small again and sitting on the back step and Deirdre is teaching me to braid so I can make Greta a friendship bracelet, but then Deirdre surprises me with one made from red and blue string which I wear till it rots off my wrist.

"Deirdre," I whisper. Then I squeal it, loud and delighted and disbelieving. "Deirdre!"

The jockey looks up, and it's her. Years older, hair shorter, but it's her, it's our Deirdre, and only Perihelion and his hulking size and fast-kicking hooves keep me from rushing over for a hug.

But Deirdre stiffens when she sees me. Her eyes get big, and she pushes down the brim of a fancy black riding helmet so her face is in shadow.

"It's Sonnia," I go on, and I am remembering how hard I cried when she stopped coming to watch us. How Greta toddled through the house for days, peeking behind doors and under our table, repeating *Deedee?* in a bewildered, hurt voice. "From Edge Lane? You used to—"

"Sonnia. Of course." Deirdre slides off Perihelion and gives me a quick, light hug across the shoulders that also guides me several paces away from the big horse and his trainers and the groom holding his halter. Lower she adds, "Yes. I remember you."

Deirdre would let us finger paint with water on the kitchen floor and eat all the blackberries we could handle from the bushes down the common. She'd be the stablemaster when Greta and I crawled around the house, pretending we were misbehaving ponies.

"*You're* the girl jockey?" I gesture around us, at the racetrack and the dozens of beautiful horses moving past. "But you weren't raised by—"

"Yes. It's me." Deirdre leans close. "People say a lot of things. Winning this spot wasn't easy, and neither is keeping it. So if you'd lower your voice, it would do me a lot of good."

She tips her chin at the knot of trainers clustered around Perihelion as they examine the stallion's forelegs and gesture to his big haunches.

I nod slowly. Deirdre grew up in darker corners with a lot less hope than I did. Bandits are criminals, but they're practically born in the saddle. The nearest to horses most lane kids get is collecting their dung for burning.

"What are you doing here?" Deirdre's voice is calm but careful, like there's a right answer and a wrong one. "You don't come to the racetrack much. That's more than obvious. So you didn't come about the cadre. Why are you here?"

Another shiver goes down my back when she says *cadre*. It's a word bandits use to describe how they ride—in a pack, like wolves. How they move together through the greenwood, day and night, watching their targets, biding their time.

I've never been to the racetrack at all. Not when I can spend hours with our ponies or the horses at the royal stables just up the road, and not when getting here involves so many tolls.

But I'm stuck on *cadre*. Shadowy figures outlined in moonlight. Hooves thudding on dirt.

Deirdre folds her arms tight, like she's a shield, and I am counting the years it's been since she stopped watching us and reckoning how she must have spent them. How girls from the lanes spend their years.

"What are you doing here?" she repeats, sharper this time, and my mouth is so dry that all I can do is gesture to Ricochet, who's standing a cautious distance from Perihelion while Paolo pats his neck in a calming, reassuring way.

"Aren't you a little young to be chasing boys?" Deirdre asks, and I scowl because it's annoying when adults say stuff like that, but then her expression softens. She smiles halfway and murmurs, "Ah. It's that horse you love."

Hardly anyone understands how much I love Ricochet, but Deirdre saw it right away. It makes me want to hug her. "He's basically my best friend. After Greta, I mean. He's a fleet horse at the royal stables, but he's going to be Perihelion's new companion."

Deirdre still looks unconvinced, and it's like I'm five again and explaining what happened to the last cookie because I add, "I'm going to buy him one day."

Her brows go up.

Right away I press my lips together. There's a reason I stopped telling people why I'm saving my coppers.

You have nowhere to keep him. Boarding will cost you a fortune. You'll soon be taking hiring fair contracts and your master and mistress won't tolerate daydreaming. You'll barely have time to ride him.

But Deirdre says, low and quiet, "They probably tell you it's foolish, right? Wanting something so big? So unimaginable? No one thinks kids like us should expect better."

Mother says I should be thankful for what I have. Mistress Crumb tells barefoot kids bound for the hiring fairs that scraps of education will improve us somehow.

Deirdre leans closer and whispers, "The only way kids like us—*girls* like us—get anything better is when we make it happen for ourselves."

She smells like expensive leather polish. Her racing silks look as soft as a horse's ear. A girl born two streets over from me, who never set foot in a schoolroom, who was no older than I am now when she started minding me and Greta and Torsten.

A girl who's achieved an unimaginable thing, telling me it's okay to want unimaginable things while standing in front of me as proof they're possible.

Deirdre steps away, toward the beautiful gold racehorse. Away from me and my thirdhand trousers with cuffs halfway up my shins.

"He's not a *want*," I say fiercely. "Ricochet's not a dessert or a jump rope. He—" I pull in a stuttery breath and blink hard. "He's waiting for me. I can't let him down."

Deirdre regards me for a moment that feels too long. Then she gestures to Ricochet and says, "He's a beauty for sure. A horse like him is going to cost a lot of coppers. Are you at the hiring fairs yet?"

I shake my head. "I'm old enough, but Father says it's better if I keep on with the pony rides."

Deirdre growls, short and wordless, and I study my feet. I'm lucky. I know I am. Plenty of parents haul their kids by the elbow to the big grassy plains on the north side of the city and make them join the long lines of available workers while magistrates and sergeants-at-law peer into their faces and demand to know if they're honest and diligent, as if there's any answer other than "Yes, m'lord."

Father says he'd never in a thousand years send us to the hiring fairs, but what he doesn't say but has to mean is he won't *send* us, but that doesn't mean we'll never have to go.

That changed for Torsten when he went to the royal stables. My brother will never have to stand in a hiring fair line and take the best contract he can get.

There's no question that in a year or two, I will.

No one's going to hire a girl for horse work, and that means a kitchen. That means scrubbing pots and floors, the only time outside on trips to the well. That means only a precious few spare coppers to keep Ricochet.

Assuming I ever get to five hundred.

Deirdre smiles sadly. "Well, I guess that's that, then. Nice seeing you."

"Wait. I don't understand. What do you mean?"

"I thought perhaps I could help you, but it looks like

I can't," she replies. "If your father doesn't want you at the hiring fairs, he'd never let you work here as a stablehand."

"At the racetrack?" I can't keep the wish out of my voice. "There's no way. I'm not from a caretaker family. The king would never approve."

"The track operates entirely separately from the royal stables. The king's racehorses win big purses and bring him lots of fame, and as long as that happens, the track stablemaster is allowed some . . . liberties." Deirdre squints. "I could make it happen, but you wouldn't get a share of the track profits. Only coppers."

Only coppers. I want to be the kind of person who has so many coppers in their pocket that they stop knowing exactly how many there are.

"How many coppers?"

"Three hundred a month."

I pull in a sharp breath. It's hard to imagine that much money in my hands all at once. Father can get the stable roof redone in slate. Greta can go to school for the whole day session.

More than that, I'll see Ricochet all the time. I'll be able to walk past his stall and pet his nose and whisper all my promises to him.

Even more than that, I'll never have to set foot at a hiring fair, and best of all, my Ricochet money would pile up so quickly, he'll be mine in a few months, way before the king might think to sell him.

"I will be the *best* stablehand!" I squeal, before I remember that I need to seem like a responsible person that can be trusted with the king's horses. "You don't even have to train me. There's been a stable full of ponies in my yard for years now, and I've been spending time with fleet horses since I was ten."

"Well, this place is nothing like the royal stables," Deirdre says, "but you'll get along fine if you do what you're told, you do it well, and you don't ask questions."

"I can do that," I say. "I absolutely can."

"You'll have to live here, too. In the bunkhouse. It's not free."

I nod. It makes sense. Torsten lives at the royal stables because horses don't care about curfew.

She peers at me. "You keep nodding. But what about your father?"

"I'll talk to him. I know he'll say yes. Mother, too. This is nothing like the hiring fairs. I mean, it's *you*. You used to change Greta's diapers. And it's three hundred coppers a month!"

Deirdre bites a thumbnail like she's deciding whether to accept a merchant's price. "I'm sticking my neck out for you because I know what it's like to be a girl in the lanes. So if you do take this job, you can't make me look bad."

"No. No. I would rather die."

If Greta were here, she'd tease me for being dramatic, but it's not every day that someone is willing to take a chance for you. Take a chance *on* you. Like there's something in you that only they can see, that they want to help along. A tiny flame that needs to be gently blown on, or a seed tucked in spring-dark earth.

Someone must have done the same for Deirdre. She must have come to the track when Mother had no more need of a babysitter and found someone to teach her to ride. She must have had her own Master Harold to bend a rule here and there.

She must want to pay it forward.

"I would rather die," I repeat, and I glance at Ricochet fierce and loving.

Deirdre smiles faintly. "Let's hope that won't be necessary."

3

"RIDER." ONE OF the trainers beckons to Deirdre, a hand on Perihelion's haunch.

"Wait here," she tells me over her shoulder, and she walks toward the men and boys around the big horse like she's always worn silks and never gone barefoot.

Without a hint of a curtsy.

"So you're staying, then?" Paolo's voice is even, almost cautious, and he makes that gesture again, bringing both hands to his belly button like he's holding reins. He stays that way, studying my face, but when I fidget with Ricochet's mane, he drops the odd pose and grins, open and friendly.

"Sorry. Didn't mean to overhear." Paolo nods at Deirdre where she's arguing with both hands at Perihelion's trainers. "I think you'll like being a stablehand for her."

I'm about to ask what he means—I'm going to be a stablehand for the racetrack, not Deirdre—but he goes on, "They're good guys over there. Marcel's a bit of a show-off. That kid's got three pairs of boots that are each worth more than a laborer makes in a month, and he wears them everywhere, even to muck stalls. Ivar's the redhead. He's gonna make a pay table for everything and he'll want you to lay wagers, but he doesn't like to lose. Just saying."

"Over where?" I ask. "Can you show me?"

"Sorry. I mostly know *of* them. I don't get to talk to them much." Paolo pats Ricochet on the shoulder. "They've got their own bunkhouse, and I have a bed next to this guy's stall."

I keep smiling somehow. That could be me, sleeping next to Ricochet and spending every moment of the day with him.

"Sonnia. This way." Deirdre appears behind me. Her cheeks are red and she's trembling like she's holding in bad words. To Paolo she says, "Perihelion's off to the track. Breezing runs. You're to ride along."

Paolo snaps a cheerful salute and swings atop Ricochet. They make a small parade up the horseway—a boy leading the riderless gold stallion, eight trainers walking two deep around him, and Paolo and Ricochet, bringing up the rear.

Wasn't Deirdre supposed to ride breezing runs on Perihelion?

But she's already halfway across the horseway, heading toward a smaller building opposite, and I hurry to follow. Inside, there's a series of empty stalls, each with a metal gate that opens onto a pasture out back, and the floor is hard-packed dirt. The whole place smells comfortingly familiar—hay and horse and yes, okay, manure.

"This is the outrider stable," Deirdre says. "Outriders are the fleet horses of the racetrack. It's not a race day, so they're all in the pasture."

Through one of the stall gates, I can see about a dozen horses grazing peacefully in a single green space bounded by four-board fences.

"Make sure you do a good job, okay? The trainers know there's a new stablehand, they know you're a girl, and they know I personally argued for you to work here."

"Got it. Got it." Thankfully, everything also looks familiar. Straw brooms with crooked wooden handles, latched feed bins, well-scrubbed water troughs, a hayloft.

"I've got business with the trainers," Deirdre says. "You can figure this out, right?"

"Yes." I say it firm and confident. Grown up, like someone who figures things out all the time.

She nods approval, and it's as good as a hug. Then she's out the door, adjusting her helmet as she goes, and after she's gone, I realize I'm not sure what I'm meant to figure out.

I haven't even told my parents where I am. Or that I've taken a job without asking them first.

There's a shuffle of feet in the horseway outside, and

a handful of kids my age trample in. They're all boys, and they stop as one when they see me.

"Are you lost?" The kid nearest to me swaggers like a rooster. His boots are dark heartbeat red, like he just walked through knee-deep blood.

"I'm the new stablehand." I brace for him to laugh or say mean things, but none of the kids even seems surprised. "Sonnia."

"You're in the right place, then." The boy next to him is all forelock, like Buttermilk, with the sort of face that seems made to smile. "We figured someone new would turn up soon to join us."

Marcel may be the show-off in blood-red boots, but there's not a ragged cuff or muddy shirt among any of these boys. They're all dressed to ride in well-made jackets that went on their backs new and breeches that don't bunch or sag.

Deirdre said the track stables had different rules than the royal stables, but clearly not that different.

A redhead who must be Ivar mutters something that ends in *girl*, and a blond kid at the edge of the group straightens abruptly. The moment we lock eyes, I realize she's not a boy, even though most of her head is shaved, all but a short section of silky palomino hair on top that slashes over her pale ears and across her eyes. I feel like a baby with my careful braids brightened up with little bows of pink cloth.

"Yeah well, Astrid doesn't count as a girl." Marcel

shoves her in a playful way, and she shoves him back. "She outrides you all the time. Are we hitting the trail or what?"

Ivar makes a rude gesture at Marcel, but they're both smiling, and I risk a smile too. Having an older brother means you're used to how some boys talk to each other. You're used to hearing things like *you don't count as a girl* as *you're one of us.*

Marcel heads up the aisle and into the field behind the stable. The others follow, and as Astrid passes, I try to catch her eye. If she's one of them, that means I could be as well.

But Astrid breezes by, calling that she has dibs on Mandalay, and I can't help but watch her go.

The Buttermilk boy is the one who stops in the doorway with a look on his face like I just dropped my ice cream. "I'm Lucan. I guess Deirdre did it again. Just left someone here and couldn't be bothered to take five minutes to show them around."

"Deirdre had things to deal with," I say stiffly, but the promise of horses is so tempting that it's not worth pointing out his rudeness. Instead I ask, "Are you really going riding? That's allowed?"

"As long as it's not race day and all the chores are finished, we can go riding when we want," Marcel replies as he carries a saddle past us and into the field.

"So you're going right now?" I can't help but grin. "Can I come?"

"Since the outriders need to spend time on the trail, the guys ride pretty much every afternoon." Lucan gestures to the pasture, where kids are catching horses or slipping bits into mouths or settling saddles onto backs. "Since you're the new stablehand, it would be weird if you *didn't* come."

I'm about to ask why the outrider horses need to spend time on the trail when Astrid looks up from shortening stirrups on a bay gelding and says, "Really, Lucan? *Guys?*"

Lucan holds his hands out in a *sorry, forgot* kind of way, and in that moment I don't care that Astrid has never had to go to bed hungry or wear hand-me-down underwear. She's done the hard work of making it easier for girls to be stablehands here. Astrid has made a path that all I have to do is follow.

"What horse should I ride?" I ask her.

Greta loves being asked for advice. She can go on forever telling you what she thinks, but Astrid isn't even looking at me. All her attention is on the saddle girth, making sure it's tight, as she murmurs, "Oh, anybody in the outrider pasture is good."

I glance over the remaining horses. They're all pretty, but sometimes it's not easy to ride a horse that isn't used to you.

"How about Hollyhock?" Lucan is holding a gray gelding by the halter. "He's got a light step and he's not one for tricks."

"Thanks." I like that Lucan talks about the outriders as if they're friends. When he offers to show me the tack room, I follow him back into the stable.

The saddle is unfamiliar, and I'm trying to work out the buckles when I notice that Ivar and Marcel keep glancing at me. The last thing I want is for them to figure I need help, so I wave in what I hope is a friendly way. Thankfully, they wave back and split apart toward their horses, but not before shaking hands like grown-ups.

Once Hollyhock is finally saddled, I lead him toward the gate where the others are waiting.

"What does your exercise course look like?" I ask, because even if I don't look the part, I can at least sound like I know what I'm doing. "I heard Marcel say we were going to hit the trail, but he can't mean that literally. Like, through the greenwood."

I grin to show I'm teasing, that I know it would be ridiculous to suggest that the king's horses risk sharp branches and exposed roots and slippery rocks and bandits waiting to knock us down and steal our mounts, but Astrid and Ivar exchange the briefest of looks.

"Actually, that's exactly what it is," Astrid replies.

I turn toward Hollyhock and slip my foot in the stirrup, but really I'm trying to work out what to say next. I love riding, but I've only ever been on a proper exercise course at the royal stables. Wide green pastures. White four-board fences running into forever.

We walk our horses in a loose cluster up the horseway. Lucan is telling me everyone's names and the horses they're riding, but I'm only partway listening because we're moving into a field that borders the greenwood and I'm still not sure this is safe.

You can tell where the clear-cutters came through long ago to create enough open space for the track complex. The edge of the greenwood rises beyond the pasture sheer and stark like the city wall. An entrance of sorts has been cleared, rounded at the top like the arched doorway of a townhouse, and the trail disappears through it into the gloom.

There's not enough room for horses side by side. One at a time, the kids enter the greenwood.

I grip and regrip the reins. I've only seen trees up close a few times, when Father and Mother have taken us for picnics outside the walls on rare days when neither of them has work and there are extra coppers for the road tolls. The size of these trees is unsettling, and so is the way their branches close in overhead, thick and leafy, blocking out the sun.

As Hollyhock moves into the dim greenwood, I flinch down in the saddle so none of the leaves touch me.

"There are no bandits this close to the walls," I whisper aloud, to myself and Hollyhock, too. "The king would never let us ride here if there was any danger to his horses."

The trail feels like the greenwood made it. Not people or even horses. You wind around huge trees, bigger around than my arms held wide, and past rocks that arrived here in ways I can't imagine.

Sometimes the trail is only wide enough for a single horse to move along comfortably, and branches tug at my tunic and drag gently over Hollyhock's rump.

Sometimes it broadens so two or three can ride alongside each other.

Sometimes I think I spot smaller trails that twist away from this one, and I'm glad that Astrid is riding several lengths ahead of me because of her red jacket that stands out so bright against the endless greens and browns.

Before long, my shoulders relax. My whole self relaxes. Even though I wish I was with Ricochet, I am never happier than when I'm riding. Even though this is not the gentle, scenic, groomed exercise course I'm used to. Ricochet and I are in the same place now, and soon I won't just be riding him. He'll be my very own forever.

Astrid's red jacket disappears around a tight curve in the trail ahead. When I round that same corner, she's gone.

I pull Hollyhock to a halt. Lucan was behind me. He'll catch up soon.

Only he doesn't. The *chirpchitter* of hidden birds and insects is the only sound. No hoofbeats. No voices.

I'm alone.

I mutter a swear and nudge Hollyhock forward. We take the tight turn slow, then climb a hill studded with rocks. At least the trail is clear and Hollyhock doesn't seem worried or scared.

We emerge in a clearing. It's lovely here, cram-packed with knee-high grass that's threaded through with wildflowers of every color. The greenwood rises on all sides like walls, solid and impenetrable.

No sign of where the trail picks up again.

No sounds but birds. No one here but us.

4

WHATEVER THIS IS, it's intentional.

Having an older brother teaches you many valuable survival skills, and one of them is *when you are being teased, getting angry only makes it worse.*

Having a younger sister teaches you to keep your head. That someone is looking up to you, and even if you're scared, you have to at least seem like you know what you're doing.

"We could go back the way we came," I say to Hollyhock, but I don't like the way it feels. Going backward.

So I *clickclick* him into motion and we walk along the edge of the meadow, where the grass turns short and croppy and the greenwood rises thick and tall. There's a break in the trees that seems like it could be the beginnings of a path, but Hollyhock grunts and shies away from it.

There's nothing about this gap that seems scary or

unwelcoming, but the path angles toward the northern end of the city, through a part of the greenwood where rangers and fleet riders have found bandit trails.

I trust Hollyhock. He's been up here a lot more times than I have, and if there's something about this maybe-trail to avoid, I'm going to listen.

Which gives me an idea. I may not know where the trail picks up, but Hollyhock might. The *guys* ride this trail every day.

I steer him to the middle of the clearing and give him his head. Hollyhock crosses the tall meadow grass and moves right for a not-quite gap between two trees, and sure enough, the trail appears just beyond.

"Good boy," I tell him, patting his neck.

We walk the path, completely alone, around trees and past fallen logs, and splash through a shin-deep stream. It would be a beautiful ride if I wasn't fighting panic. If I could think of anything but bandits lurking behind every tree, or being lost here forever and my parents never knowing what became of me.

Ahead, there's a mouthful of brightness that can only be daylight. I rush Hollyhock into a trot, and soon we emerge from the trees into a strip of cleared space behind a big fenced pasture. Beyond the field, I can see the track grandstand, and beyond, tiny in the distance, the city wall of Mael Dunn with the castle rising on its mound.

The racing complex. Astrid letting her gelding browse.

Marcel and Ivar craning their necks toward the green-wood. The other stablehands gathered around a water trough.

We made it. I slide down from the saddle onto shaking legs and give Hollyhock a long hug.

When I let go and turn from him, Ivar and Marcel are peering into my face. Brows furrowed. Jostling to get closer. Like they'd been worried and wanted to be sure I was okay.

Having an older brother means you know sometimes boys show you their feelings instead of telling you, and I fumble for a way to say thank you without actually saying it, which would make things weird.

Then Ivar laughs, long and cackling, and holds out his hand at Marcel, who starts grumblingly digging through his pockets. Marcel pulls out a handful of coppers, pokes through them, then pours them into Ivar's palm.

I'm staring. Openmouthed. Then I snap, "Are you *wagering* on me?"

"Five coppers that you'd turn back." Ivar pockets the money. "Three that you'd finish the ride, but you'd be crying."

So it was a prank. I know for a fact that I wasn't the last in line. Lucan should have come up behind me.

He's in on this.

Having an older brother *and* a younger sister means you're pretty hard to tease, but this doesn't feel like teasing.

"All that just from looking at me?" I smile to show I refuse to be upset. "You didn't even check my teeth or see a breezing run."

Ivar laughs and leads his horse toward the trough. The other boys don't look happy to see him. One pulls out a coin purse before he even arrives.

If they're paying Ivar, it means they bet against me. They thought I'd turn back or straggle in crying.

They clearly don't know what it takes to grow up in the lanes.

I *clickclick* to Hollyhock and lead him in the direction I saw Marcel and Astrid go, hopefully toward the outrider stable. The gelding's footfalls are rhythmic and calming, and I put myself back in order.

I was never in any danger. Hollyhock knew the way the whole time. It was just a prank.

Which means I doubt the stablehands will invite me to go riding again. A prank is only funny the first time, before the mark knows to expect it.

I'm not sure I'd go if they offered. Not if this is how it's going to be.

I pay no attention to the hooves echoing behind me till they stop at my elbow. Lucan slides down from his mare and walks beside us.

"How much did Ivar cut you in for?" I ask. "Or did you do it just for fun?"

Lucan flinches. "Did you ever think I was hanging back to make sure you got through safely? That if you did turn around, there'd be someone to guide you? Happens more often than you'd think."

"You could have ridden with me."

"You'd have never heard the end of it. If it turns out that you keep riding with us, you don't want any of the guys—or Astrid—thinking you can't handle the trail. Do you?"

If it turns out that you keep riding with us. I peer at him, not sure what to make of all the maybes in it. "Well. All right. Thank you."

"Besides, I learned my lesson a while ago when it comes to Ivar. Guy doesn't like to lose."

Paolo said something similar. "Lose what? Wagers?"

"Anything."

When we arrive at the outrider stable, a few stablehands are already untacking their horses and giving them a currying. Hollyhock's coat is warm to the touch, not too hot, so he doesn't need any more walking to cool down. I give him some water, then remove his saddle and bridle, wipe them clean, and put them where they go in the tack room. Then I get a wooden box of grooming brushes and set to work.

Stiff bristle. Soft bristle. Brush and detangle.

My eyes sting, but the worst thing I can do now is let slip how much their prank hurt.

I shouldn't be too surprised. Marcel, Ivar, Astrid— those kids are clearly from caretaker families, and they took one look at my thirdhand barn jacket and falling-apart work boots and realized I would never belong.

Girls like me scrub washbasins in houses that kids like them grew up in. We bring their lamb chops and soap their underwear.

We lead their pony rides.

When Hollyhock's coat is shining, I turn him loose into the outrider pasture. The big green space backs to the three-quarters turn of the racetrack, and at the farthest corner, there's a shelter where horses can stand to get out of the weather.

The stablehands are in there now, sitting on upturned buckets and eating something from a bag they're handing around.

I could quit. There's nothing wrong with giving pony rides. Buttermilk is the best pony in Mael Dunn, and one copper in every twenty is a sure thing.

Only maybe I'm Deirdre's big ask, like Torsten was Master Harold's. Maybe she convinced the trainers—the track stablemaster himself—to give me a chance.

I glance at the sun. If I start now, I can get home by supper and tell my parents everything, then walk through the night and be back in time for morning chores.

I'm heading up the horseway toward the city gate when someone shouts my name. Marcel waves from the pasture fence like he wants me to come over. I really don't have time for someone who wagered on me crying, but I veer off the horseway and trot near.

"Going to tattle on us?" His voice is as bland as porridge.

"For what?" I smile. "I got to go riding today. The worst day in the saddle is still a good day."

"Then why are you heading toward the track sidelines?"

"I'm not. I'm going to my house." I nod at the city walls. "I didn't know I was taking a stablehand job when I got here this morning. My parents will be worried if I just disappear."

Marcel nods slowly. "Good. Come with me."

"What? Why?"

"It works better when everyone's in." He points at the pasture shelter where the other stablehands are gathered.

Whatever. I'm not falling for another prank. It's already going to take hours to get home through the lanes. They can hardly be called roads, twisting and dead-ending every which way through neighborhoods into alleys and around shop fronts, but unlike the toll roads that cut straight through town, they don't cost anything to use.

"Sonnia!" Marcel tosses me something small and metal. A toll road token. These might be made of cheap tin, but each one gets you inside the walls and through as many tollbooths as you need. I'd be home in the time it takes to cook rice.

I'm stunned silent. I just met this kid and a gift like this feels out of all measure.

"Will you come now?" he asks, and I nod numbly. I hold the token tight in my fist as I climb the fence and cross the pasture toward the stablehands in the shelter.

When we get there, Marcel takes a seat on the only empty bucket, and I'm left standing awkwardly in the big space that passes for the entryway.

"There are two things you need to do to join the junior racing cadre," Marcel says. "You ride to win and you go the way the wind blows."

"Which is why there's a test," Lucan adds helpfully. "Which you passed, by the way."

Cadre. Like they're bandits. These kids can't be foolhardy enough to be given the chance to work at the racetrack and throw that word around like it's meaningless.

"You didn't turn back when you were alone and you didn't run squealing to adults," Astrid clarifies. "If you hadn't passed, we wouldn't be talking now."

"I didn't cry, either." I glance pointedly at Ivar.

"Ahhh, that was just a side bet." He makes a *no big deal* gesture. "Crying doesn't disqualify you from the cadre. It just happens often enough that it's worth making a few coppers on."

"I thought for sure a girl would cry," mutters Roland, who's glumly toying with a sagging money pouch.

"Junior racing . . . cadre?" I repeat, just to be sure.

Astrid nods. "We're training to ride racehorses for the king. All of us have our eye on a spot among the king's jockeys."

"And a room in the jockey house, and a spot on the pay table," Marcel adds.

Lucan must figure I'm confused instead of skeptical, because he says, "There's a public list of which jockeys are riding which horses, and what odds they have to win, place, or show in a race. That's the pay table. Jockeys get a cut of any purse their horse earns."

"There's a bonus, too, if a horse wins with long odds." Ravik has the aristocratic down-the-nose look of a prize thoroughbred. "When the king wins big, he does not forget his jockeys."

I turn the toll road token over and over between my fingers. It gives me time to think.

Deirdre said something about a cadre when I arrived. That I couldn't have come about it because I don't often come to the track.

If there's a group of kids actively training to be jockeys, it would explain how Deirdre came to be standing where she is now. When she watched us, she barely knew which end of a horse the food went in.

Maybe this is what she meant. She did say that the track stables work differently than the royal stables. Maybe she thought I'd come to learn to ride racehorses for the king.

"We want you to ride with us." Marcel glances around the group. "Like I said, it works so much better when everyone's in."

"Aren't we stablehands?" I ask, but the idea of riding

racehorses for the king is whispering through my head now. All of Mael Dunn cheering as I wave from the back of a dancing thoroughbred with a wreath of winners' roses around his neck. The king himself grinning like a month of paydays from his viewing box and his daughters clapping wildly, begging to meet me.

Ivar is sitting in a slant of shadow. When he shifts on his crate, there's a faint clink of coppers in his pockets. "No reason we can't do both."

He's gonna make a pay table for everything. He doesn't like to lose.

They might be wagering on me again right now. How long the lane kid will believe there's such a thing as the junior racing cadre, and how long she'll believe she's a part of it.

A part of *them*.

"Let me think about it." I nod politely to Marcel, sweep a bland smile around the circle of stablehands, then head toward the horseway without looking back.

5

FATHER AND MOTHER are quiet for a long time when I tell them.

Mother is worried I'll be hungry and have nowhere to sleep. I tell her how all the stablehands are around my age and there's a bunkhouse just for us, how there's a cookhouse right across from it where everyone at the track gets three meals a day.

Father is unhappy that I'll have to quit school, but I remind him that I can read and write okay, that he and Mother have more than gotten their money's worth.

Mother says yes first, after I tell her it was Deirdre who offered me the job. She sighs and says, "I've always felt terrible about letting the poor girl go like I did. I knew she needed the money, but . . ."

But so did we is what Mother means but doesn't want to say.

"Didn't Deirdre once let me eat an entire stick of

butter?" Greta asks without looking up from her book.

I frown at her, trying to send a sister mind message that now is not the best time to bring that up, but she just tips the pages toward the fire to get more light.

Father says yes only after I tell him how much money I'll be able to send home each month. The coppers from pony rides are the difference between having enough and having to sacrifice, but half of three hundred will make up for my share.

"Half of three hundred is a hundred and fifty." Greta turns a page. "It's not your reading or writing you should be worried about."

"That's what I keep you around for," I reply in a teasing singsong, but she doesn't smirk or stick out her tongue. She just keeps reading.

I blink rapidly, stung. I wait for any kind of response, but after a few long moments, I quietly climb into the loft to pack.

I was only half-joking. I spent the whole walk home trying to do the figuring, but I kept tripping up on half of three hundred. Thanks to Greta, I know that every month I can send a hundred and fifty coppers home and save that many for Ricochet.

Which means that by the end of the summer racing season, I can count dinars into Master Harold's hand, then put a red bridle on Ricochet to tell the world he's mine.

Once I've bundled my clothing, I tuck the little bag

that holds my Ricochet money into the inside pocket of my barn jacket, where it rests against my heart like a promise. Buying him is within reach now, and my sister is right. Knowing what I have makes him seem so much closer.

Greta is quiet all through supper. She's quiet as she piles the dishes into the washtub. Without a word, I take one handle and help her carry them out back to the pump.

"Are you mad?" I ask quietly.

"No." She flutters half a sidelong smile as she scrapes the plates. "Of course not."

"I mean, if Mistress Crumb offered you a job as an apprentice teacher, I'd be thrilled."

"I know."

"I can't turn down a chance to spend my life with horses," I whisper. "It's not going to happen any other way."

Greta wrings out the dishcloth, not disagreeing. She's still a few years away from the hiring fairs, but she's not a fool. Both of us know Mistress Crumb has no need of an apprentice, and even if she did, it would be someone from the academy for townhouse girls. Someone highborn but with a streak of charity in her, someone who considers working with kids like us *a calling*.

Mother and Father both try to convince me to spend the night—*just one more night with us all together; there are all sorts of shifty types in the lanes after dark*—but it'll definitely make Deirdre look bad if the new stablehand isn't there for evening chores *and* morning chores.

"Someone gave me a toll road token," I tell them, which is technically true. They don't have to know I already spent it getting here. "Those streets are well lit and patrolled."

I hug them both twice, and pull Greta into the embrace as well. Then I shoulder my bundle and head toward the track.

I've rarely been out after dark, and never by myself. The sky above is black but thick with stars. I pull my cloak tight around me, blank my gaze, and break into a trot, threading through the warren of little streets toward the racetrack.

Getting anywhere through the lanes takes forever in daylight, but at night it's even harder. The moon rises slow and lazy over the city wall, as big as a dinner plate. When it's up like this, silver light pours everywhere, and I'm glad for the way it brightens up the scarier corners and dead ends where I have to backtrack.

Finally—*finally*—I emerge near the city wall, and I have to wake up the gatemen to let me through. The track is still and silent in a glorious pour of silver light, snug and tidy, almost tucked in, and that's when I realize I have nowhere to sleep. There's a bunkhouse for stablehands, but no one showed me where it was. Not any of the kids. Not Deirdre.

I know someone with big, comfortable quarters,

though. Ricochet. It's not the safest thing in the world, sleeping in a stall near a horse, but I don't have much choice. Besides, Paolo is in charge of Ricochet, and he won't tell anyone if I sleep there one night. He'll probably think it's funny.

As I'm walking up the horseway, there's a shift in the shadows near the outrider stable, and Ivar steps into the silvery light leading Tempest. He puts one foot in the stirrup, swings into the saddle, and hurries the horse away.

Something terrible must have happened. A disaster of some kind. A fire, or a bandit raid. There's no other reason anyone might bring out one of the king's horses in the middle of the night.

But if something terrible happened, the track would never be this quiet. Neither would the city. The big bell tower on the common would be ringing an alarm, and the streets would be filled with people and constables and rangers.

If a rider was needed, someone at the royal stables would be saddling a fleet horse.

And it wouldn't be a kid.

Whatever Ivar's doing, there's no way he has permission. No one so much as trims the hoof of one of the king's horses without his say-so.

Another horse clatters from the outrider stable into the horseway. A bay gelding with a white star, Ravik on his back. Then Astrid on Jubilee. Dressed in black, all of them. They disappear one at a time into the night.

None of them pay me any attention. They move like they've done this a thousand times. Peter and Roland, each with horses I don't recognize, with flashy piebald markings. When Lucan appears with a little brown mare, I glide through the darkness and put myself at her head just as he's bringing the bit to her mouth.

"Sonnia! You're in!" He grins like he just learned there's meat for supper. "They weren't going to put you on the pay table, but Ivar talked them into it. That guy can read a room, and he can read people, too. I'm kind of jealous, truth be told."

"In?" I grind my voice down to a fierce whisper. "In what? What's going on?"

"In the junior racing cadre." Lucan pats the mare's neck.

I'm floundering. "But what . . . what is . . . ?"

"Sonnia's here?" Marcel steps out of the stable leading Gladiola. "Good thing I didn't lay coppers down on it. Ivar's going to have a field day." To me he says, "Grab a horse and saddle up. You're lucky I'm dropping the kerchief or you'd have missed the whole Ride. No one's going to make allowances for you just because you're new."

"Hold on." I'm fighting for calm. "First off, no one's saying I'm joining the junior racing cadre. I'm still not convinced the whole thing's not a giant prank, but if it is, it's just gotten a whole lot less funny."

"A prank?" Lucan sounds hurt. "No, of course not. You're a really good rider and we want you in the junior racing cadre. You'll be great at the Night Ride."

"Are you *joking*?" I splutter. "We can't go riding now!"

"Horses have good night vision. They can see the trail way better than we can, especially when the moon is up."

I go cold all over. "Trail? You mean you're riding horses on the same trail we rode earlier?"

The one with the tight turns and the steep hills. The hidden hollows and creeks with rocks that can turn a horse's ankle. With boulders that can crack a hoof. With low branches and thorns that can carve scratches into legs or a chest or put out an eye.

"There's no way you're allowed to do this," I say through my teeth.

"It's not a race day, is it? Chores are done?" Gladiola is dancing in place, and Marcel turns her in a gentle circle to keep her contained. "You coming?"

"No. Never. This is wrong." I hug myself, shaking my head again and again like it will stop them.

"Pity." Marcel lets Gladiola loose and she leaps forward. Soon they're gone, across the horseway and toward the dark field.

"Sonnia?" Lucan says softly. "Are you sure? The Night Ride isn't as bad as you think. It's actually kind of fun. You've got good instincts. You wouldn't be here if you didn't. Not everyone gets a chance like this."

The junior racing cadre is not a prank. That means there really is a group of kids who are learning to ride racehorses for the king, and Deirdre was probably one of them once upon a time.

Lucan must realize I'm not moving, because he swings onto Calpurnia. "I'm sorry. I can't fall off the pay table. Not even for a week. I've got to go."

They hurtle away, and in moments, all is still again. The outrider stable. The horseway. All edged in the kind of bright silver light that makes everything easy to see.

Except why these kids are doing something so dangerous.

Not just because a horse could snap an ankle or take a sharp branch to the eye and have to be put down and mourned. Not just because a kid could be thrown and break a leg. Or their neck.

Because if the king had even the smallest suspicion that one of his horses was in danger, he'd have a fire kindled on the town common. The bell would be rung to bring out everyone in Mael Dunn, and every last one of the stablehands—the junior racing cadre—would be marched there in chains. There'd be a long metal rod in the fire, and at the end, heating till it's red-hot, would be a brand the size of an apple: *HH*.

HH for horse harm.

If the kids were lucky, they'd be made to put out

their right hands, and the glowing metal would be pressed there while they screamed and screamed till the flesh seared.

If they weren't, if the harm was bad enough, the brand would go on their faces. Cheek or forehead, depending on the harm and the horse and how deeply the king loved it.

At the end of the branding, each harmer of horses would be dragged to the city gates and put out for good, never allowed to return.

It wouldn't matter that they were kids. Anyone who mistreats the king's horses gets the brand and exile.

I'm waiting in the outrider stable when the stablehands get back. Perched on a bale of straw, stiff and rigid like a bridle that's been left to dry sweat-soaked. From up the horseway they come, hooves clopping, and a low, excited murmur of voices.

". . . know better than to rush her across the creek . . ."

". . . placed second, for the first time in at *least* three Rides . . ."

". . . not limping, is he? Because they keep saying how the animal hospital won't . . ."

Lucan is the first through the door, and I stand up. It's too dark to see his face, but his voice is cautiously cheerful. "Sonnia, hey. You should have come. You missed Astrid *smoking* past Marcel in the meadow and beating him to the drop going down the path."

I turn the safety lamps up a click, then fold my arms. "Please tell me this isn't what it looks like. Because I've been sitting here for the last several hours trying to think through what it is, and nothing I come up with is good."

"It's five dinars, baby. Winner's purse." Ivar ambles into a span of lamplight and jingles a handful of palm-sized coins. I can't take my eyes off them.

Five dinars. Two months' wages, right in his hand.

"I'm not your baby," I growl, but a purse is something that comes to the winner of a race, and all at once I'm struggling to breathe because the Night Ride isn't just a really, *really* bad idea of going on a trail ride in the middle of the night.

They weren't going to put you on the pay table.

If there's a pay table and a purse for the winner—

"It's a race," I rasp. "You're racing horses without permission on the trail at night. Not just tonight, either. You do this all the time."

"Of course the Night Ride is a race." Roland is clearly trying to keep the *well, duh* out of his voice. "It's the junior *racing* cadre, isn't it? Winner's purse is nice, but there's fifty coppers for any rider who finishes fair."

"We don't do this all the time either," Lucan says reassuringly. "Once a week when the moon is up and it's bright enough to see."

Astrid has crosstied Jubilee in her stall, and now she's

pulling off the mare's bridle and stationing a bucket of water at her feet.

"You can't give her all that water if she's just been racing!" I make a panicky rush toward the stall, but Astrid holds me off with a gentle but firm stiff-arm.

"She's been walked cool, all right? Dang."

I slump against the wall, my shoulders digging into a wooden rack of grooming tools, and I watch the stable-hands untack and turn out the horses they've been riding. They move quick and deliberate, as if they're used to doing this in the dark.

They probably are.

"Why are you doing this?" I ask quietly. "Don't you know what would happen if anyone found out?"

"Nobody will find out," Marcel replies as he hauls a saddle past me to the tack room, "because no one's going to say anything."

I straighten. "What makes you think I won't?"

"Why would you?" He pauses in the doorway. "You're here, aren't you? I thought you wanted to join the junior racing cadre. That means going where the wind blows."

"It has to stop." I lift my chin. "Someone could get hurt. *Horses* could get hurt."

"The Night Ride's not going to stop," Ravik says in a kind but matter-of-fact way. "The best thing to do is get something out of it along with the rest of us."

For a long moment I imagine having actual dinars.

Feeling my pocket push out because I have money enough to make choices.

How it would feel to proudly hand my parents enough to pay their rent in advance, or better still, move to a safer neighborhood.

How it would feel to stand before Master Harold and count dinars into his hand one at a time until Ricochet was my very own.

"What if you get caught?" I ask, low and fierce. "Sooner or later, one of the trainers is going to find out. He'll tell the track stablemaster, who'll go right to the king!"

"That's unlikely." Ivar leads Tempest to the gate and turns her loose into the pasture. "I'll take your money if you want to put some down on it, though. Let's say . . . ten thousand to one?"

I don't know a lot about wagering, but I do know that the higher the odds, the more likely that you're just giving your coppers away.

Ivar is so sure. But if the Night Ride happens all the time, someone's bound to investigate a lantern bobbing in the dark or a clatter of movement when everything should be still, or notice sweaty horses in the morning.

Still, I shake my head once, curtly.

"Anyone show you the bunkhouse?" Lucan asks, and he gestures to my bundle of clothes from home still over my shoulder.

If he didn't sound so kind, I would have told him off,

that I want nothing to do with him or any of these kids, but I can barely stay on my feet. I shake my head, and soon we're walking up the moonlit horseway toward a loaf-shaped building with a tin roof.

The door opens onto a long, dusty hallway that smells like hay, and at the far end there's a big window with real glass. A panel of silver streams through that window, lighting up the hallway enough for me to see the outlines of doorways, six on each side.

Lucan pushes open the door to the last room on the left, and there's just enough moonlight to make out a narrow pallet set on a wooden bedframe, and an apple crate that looks like it could be a table, or a chair, or a footrest, or a storage trunk. A metal key is hanging from the lock, and Lucan hands it to me.

I murmur *thank you*, and the moment he's gone, I turn the key behind me and collapse onto the bed. The bag of Ricochet coppers in my barn jacket digs into my ribs, and I wriggle out of the coat and drape it over me like a blanket. The pallet smells musty, but my eyes are dragging closed.

I own one of Ricochet's hooves. If I do what I'm told and do it well and don't ask questions, he'll be all mine by summer's end.

That's the only thing that matters.

6

THE NEXT MORNING, I sit on the edge of my bed for a long time. I know I need to get moving. I can smell the cookhouse and breakfast from here—pancakes and honey syrup—but my whole stomach is tumbling.

I don't know how to face them. What to say.

In the cookhouse, after I get a big plate of food, I scan for a corner to eat in, but Marcel waves me over to the table where the stablehands are sitting. There's already a spot for me when I arrive, between Lucan and Roland. The kids are laughing and talking over each other, asking how I slept, apologizing for how bare the bunkhouse is, pretending to steal one another's bacon.

It's like the Night Ride never happened.

I eat till I'm full while they tell stories about going on post parade with the outriders, the crowd roaring and the racehorses prancing and the jockeys crouched up on racing saddles like graceful sculptures.

It seems like a strange way to learn to ride racehorses, but maybe it makes more sense when you're doing it.

When we go to the outrider stable for morning chores, I head into the tack room to get started cleaning saddles and bridles. Everything should be stiff and sweaty, put away in the dark last night, but I stop short in the doorway.

It's all clean. Every loop of leather is hung up dry and tidy. The saddles perched on their sawhorses, the damp pads in a wicker laundry basket.

Of course someone sneaked in and cleaned everything. The last thing the junior racing cadre wants is to get caught.

I go outside to drain the troughs and pump fresh water. Astrid comes to help me, but all I can think to say has to do with the Night Ride. How wrong it is, how dangerous, and she's not going to want to hear it.

So I just work the pump and keep quiet.

I do what I'm told, and that's barn chores in the outrider stable. Rattling grain into feed bins and shoveling manure out of stalls and the pasture. Curry and comb and pick hooves. Stiff bristle. Soft bristle. Brush and detangle.

I do it well. None of the outrider horses is Ricochet, but I get to know them, and it's not long before I love them, too.

Playful Gladiola, who loves to pull the cloth ties off the ends of my braids while I'm cleaning her hooves.

Shy, sweet Mandalay, who will nose his big head under my elbow to get me to scritch him.

Hollyhock, who likes to play keep-away in the pasture when it's time for grooming. He reminds me of our pony Boris with his cheerful, can-do nature, and when it's time for trail rides in the afternoons, he's the horse I choose.

I will never do the Night Ride, but I can't pass up any chance to spend an hour or two in the saddle.

Every day the trail becomes less scary, and I start to notice where the paths go, where giant boulders create bends in the trail, and where the uphill stretches are rocky and where they're smooth.

Each time we take different little half-trails, curving around new trees and past different bushes and rocks, but pretty soon I'm not worried. We always end up in the same place—that long straight stretch that leads to the back pasture gate. Besides, Hollyhock knows the way, and it's not long before I do too.

"Race day tomorrow," Lucan says one afternoon as we're turning the outrider horses into their pasture. "So no trail ride. But the good news is that after the outriders are bathed and braided in the morning, we're free to do what we like."

What I like is going on trail rides, but I don't say as much. Besides, tomorrow will be Ricochet's big day, out on the track with Perihelion. Even if I'm not the one who gets to ride Ricochet, I want to see him, and I want to see everyone admiring him. I've also heard Deirdre will be riding Perihelion, and maybe she'll wave to me in the crowd.

I brighten and ask, "Can we watch the races? Does it cost anything?"

"Ah." Lucan frowns like I asked to drink paint. "I guess."

I must look alarmed, because he goes on, "There's no admission fee for track workers and we're allowed to watch. It's just that none of us want to."

"Why not?"

"Stablehands either win the chance to ride or we . . ." Lucan runs a hand through his long hair, then spins it into a knot by his pale neck. "It's hard, is all. There are ten of us in the cadre, but only six at a time get to go on post parade with the outriders on the track with the racehorses."

As he says it, I picture myself on Hollyhock's back, mere lengths from Ricochet, all of us sharing the excitement of the moments before a race.

"So do you take turns, or . . . ?" I trail off as Lucan shakes his head.

"The top six finishers," he replies quietly. "You ride to win. Or you sit out race day."

Cadre is a word bandits use to describe how they ride—in a group, tight together. Seems like the last thing you'd want in a junior racing cadre is anything that makes it hard to stick together.

Race day dawns clear and glorious, and I hurry through morning chores because the stablehands are in charge of making six of the outriders shine. We lead each horse onto a concrete slab near the pump, pour water over them, then towel them off.

Across the horseway, an army of grooms in royal purple are sprucing up the companion horses. Ricochet is among them, looking as lovely as ever. Paolo spots me and waves, and I slip across the horseway to say hello.

"Perihelion's in the last race, along with a gorgeous brown mare belonging to the duke," he tells me. "Word is that the king has wagered the duke a basket of fine cheeses that Helie will leave that mare in the dust. The duke has put up a barrel of wine."

"Really? Not money?"

Paolo shakes his head. "The king thinks people should watch horses run because it's exciting. He doesn't like the idea of wagering on the outcome. There's a minimum of fifty dinars at the track betting window just to keep people from doing it."

Fifty dinars. If I had that kind of money, I sure wouldn't waste it on a guess.

Lucan is waving me over, so I say goodbye to Paolo and get back to work. Pretty soon the outrider horses are ready to go. Six kids wearing their best riding gear mount up and join the procession toward the receiving barn, where the racehorses will wait for their turn to run. Ivar is there, and Marcel and Roland and two boys I don't know well.

Astrid is among them, wearing her red jacket. All six are having a cheerful debate over which trainer has the most ear hair, and my heart goes *pang* because watching her makes it all feel so possible.

I put my hand over my Ricochet coppers in my inner pocket and press them close.

Sure enough, once the outriders have left for the receiving barn, the remaining stablehands drift in all directions. I wash up at the pumphouse, then head straight for the races.

The track complex is busier than I've ever seen it, and there's a lively festival air to the place. Dozens of horses from nearby kingdoms have arrived to take part in the races, and it feels like there are ten times as many people. Someone is playing a lute, and there are carts where you can buy candied apples and fried things that smell heavenly.

I slip past shoulders and dodge under elbows and squeeze myself in a gap near the rail. If I crane my neck, I can see the king in his royal viewing box draped with the city crest. His daughters are there too, one on either side of him, and they're throwing flowers down to people below. They're about my age, with black hair in long braids like mine, and I feel a little better about not having a sassy cut like Astrid's.

The races are as exciting as I hoped they'd be. Everyone holds their breath as the horses gather at the chalk line, and you jump when the starting bell goes off.

Your fingers sting as you grip the rail, and you can feel the drum of hooves as the pack comes around the turns.

At some point you realize you're yelling, and everyone around you is yelling, and when a horse thunders past the finish line ahead of the rest, your whole heart leaps because what you just saw was simply, gloriously breathtaking.

A bay gelding from a neighboring kingdom wins the first race by almost three lengths. He has the look of a cart horse, all raw bones and a straggly tail, but he shatters the competition. The king's black mare wins the second race, but only by half a length. The anointed sovereign of Mael Dunn leaps to his feet cheering like a prizefighter when she flies across the chalk line. A white mare wins the next race, and a flashy roan stallion the one after that, and then it's time.

The last race, starring Perihelion.

Horses from other kingdoms come out one at a time from an entryway and walk along the track. People applaud and cheer and comment aloud on who has the best chances of winning. I spot Astrid in her red jacket alongside one of them, riding Gladiola, and there's Marcel on Mandalay.

But the moment Ricochet steps onto the dirt, I can't look away from him. Paolo waves once to the grandstand, cheerful, but then he's all business, keeping Ricochet walking between Perihelion and the crowd, because it's obvious that Perihelion needs calming.

The gold stallion is dancing all over the place, tossing his head, kicking air. Deirdre on his back can hardly keep him moving forward, and this only makes the crowd more excited. The cheering and noise get louder.

Perihelion half-rears, then swerves toward Ricochet. Paolo can't move out of the way in time, and the horses sideswipe hard into each other. The stallion leaps forward and his rein snaps and he takes off at a bucking canter-gallop that lasts until well beyond the first quarter turn, until Deirdre can lean forward enough to grab the flapping piece of broken rein and Astrid can match their pace on Gladiola and help her bring Perihelion to a staggering, kicking halt.

The king is on his feet. He's pressing both hands over his mouth like someone just peed in his cider. His elder daughter is covering her eyes and the younger is looking away like she's embarrassed.

Perihelion is whisked into the receiving barn and fitted with a new bridle, but it doesn't matter. The duke's brown mare wins handily, and Perihelion comes last by almost ten lengths.

The crowd cheers its heart out, and nearby the line judges prepare a carpet of daisies to drape over the winning horse's withers. Deirdre guides Perihelion down the backstretch on his cooling lap. The other horses are well beyond the three-quarters turn, and the winner is already moving toward the victory circle.

The companion horses are waiting at the gate to the receiving barn, and as each racehorse arrives, they pair off and walk through together.

Ricochet isn't there, though, and Perihelion walks in alone.

7

NO ONE IS sure how they tell time, but the outrider horses are always waiting in their stalls for morning feeding. They're allowed to come and go from the pasture, even at night, and walking into the stable every morning and breathing in their horsey smell and giggling at how impatient they all seem is a gift I get every day.

But today there are only eleven pushy noses hovering over feed boxes. In the pasture, a cider-colored blur shifts in the shelter by the three-quarters turn. It's Jubilee.

When I get nearer, I notice she's holding a foot off the ground.

I get a hoof pick, then run a hand gently down her leg, lift the hoof, and turn it toward me. There's a bit of crud, which I gently flip out with the pick, but right away it's pretty clear what the problem is.

A crack. By the looks of it, one that hasn't been treated properly.

Supposedly there's an outrider stablemaster, but I have yet to meet him, so instead I find Lucan tossing soiled bedding onto the manure sledge.

"What do we do when one of the horses is hurt?" I ask.

His smile freezes. "How hurt?"

"A cracked hoof." I gesture at Jubilee hunching beneath the shelter. "Nothing urgent, but it still needs looking at."

Lucan's whole body relaxes. "Right. Sure. I'll take care of it, okay?"

I thank him, but it's hard to go back to work even though horses get little injuries all the time. They're not exactly careful.

After breakfast and chores, there's not much to do till our afternoon trail ride. Some of the boys kick a ball around the empty field in front of the greenwood. Marcel and Astrid like to read. They can sit for hours in the shade in front of the bunkhouse quietly turning pages, and occasionally trading books.

For kids who are supposedly learning to ride racehorses for the king, the junior racing cadre doesn't spend a lot of time near jockeys, or the track, or the trainers, or the horses themselves.

No one has said a word to me about the Night Ride for a while now. No invitations. No pleas. No demands.

I can almost forget it's still happening.

I spend my free time leaning on the four-board fence surrounding Ricochet's private pasture. There are too many racehorse caretakers around for me to call him over, but no one seems to mind me watching him.

Ricochet's not outside today, and when I peek into the barn, there's a bustle of grooms and horseboys crowding the aisle. They must still be trying to figure out what happened with Perihelion last race day. Mixing him different feed. Giving him more vitamins. Trying out new pairs of blinkers.

I drift into the horseway. If Ricochet is busy, Paolo will be too. I could ask to join the ball game, and the stablehands would probably let me play, but it feels uncomfortable somehow. Joining them for anything.

It works so much better when everyone's in.

From the road, I spot Jubilee in the shelter. Her hoof is still up. Her nose pointed at the ground. There must be a homemade foot soak that could help—

"Hey!"

I spin around at the thunder of hooves. Ricochet is galloping full tilt out of the racehorse barn. He looks terrified, snort-whinnying with every step, eyes wild. Paolo sprints after him, a bridle dragging in the dust, and somewhere in the barn Perihelion is screaming and neighing like Ricochet just cheated at cards.

I hurry toward Ricochet with my arms raised, trying to get him to slow down. He angles past me and leaps over the four-board fence and into the outrider pasture. The other horses look up, everything from curious to alert to wary, but Ricochet drops into a canter and heads to the far end of the pasture. The others drift away from him as if they know he needs space.

"What's going on?" I demand as Paolo trails to a stop in front of the pasture fence.

Paolo's shoulders are shaking as he holds a hand to his mouth, and I edge close, concerned. When lane boys cry, they tend to do it in private.

But Paolo isn't crying. He's laughing.

"Good riddance!" Perihelion's head trainer is broad like a draft horse's rear end, and he lurches out of the racehorse barn with a handful of leg wrappings in one fist and a broken lead rein in the other. He flings the scrap of leather into the horseway, in the direction Ricochet fled. "I'll have you sent to the butchery pens, you nag!"

I flinch. The constables are always threatening the butchery pens when they check and recheck our pony ride license.

Paolo steps into the trainer's way, still giggling. "Come now, you have to admit a horse being bitten on the backside is pretty funny."

"Funny?" The trainer twists the leg wrappings till his knuckles turn white. "After what happened at the track? Do you have any idea how bad Ricochet made the king look? A racehorse worth five thousand dinars, losing by ten lengths!"

But—Ricochet didn't do anything! Perihelion was the one who collided with *him.*

"That wretched animal is finished as a companion horse," the trainer growls. "I want him out of my barn and out of my sight."

Paolo gestures grandly to Ricochet in the outrider pasture. "Already done."

The trainer mutters something full of swears, turns on his heel, and storms back to the racehorse barn, where Perihelion has quieted and the crowd of grooms and undertrainers has grown.

Paolo turns to me with a grin. "Poor Ricochet. We should give him a treat. It must be rough, being dismissed. Even if the job stinks."

I'm not used to someone else caring about Ricochet. Not grooming or feeding him, but how he feels. If he's happy, or needs attention or cheering up.

I like it, though. It's the same as having a friend in common. "I'll show you where we keep the apples."

The outrider stable is dim and cool in the heat of the day. I open the hinged lid of the apple bin and choose several of the small green ones that Ricochet likes best. We cross the pasture, and Ricochet sees us and comes over. Paolo pets and fusses over him in a way I thought would annoy me, but makes me smile.

"I guess this means you're dismissed too." I offer an apple to Paolo. "Need a treat?"

He laughs. "Nah. Perihelion will have a new companion before the day is out, and that means I'll have a new friend too. Best get back to it."

Paolo takes the apple anyway and tosses it from one hand to the other as he heads toward the racehorse barn.

"I guess this means you're going back to the royal stables," I say to Ricochet as he crunches his apple. "Back to being a fleet horse. But you know what? Everyone should be gathering soon for the trail ride. We could go together, before you head home."

Ricochet noses me, and even though Paolo probably already groomed him today, I grab a soft bristle brush and run it over his coat to help calm him.

"I know you didn't do anything to Perihelion at the racetrack," I murmur. "It's not your fault he lost. Someone's got to be blamed, though. It's never someone highborn."

When Ricochet seems happier, I turn him loose to graze, and I find some bits to scrub. It's satisfying, making things in a stable clean and perfect.

Before long, there's a chatter of voices in the horseway, and the stablehands appear in their riding clothes.

I join them in the pasture and put two fingers to my mouth and whistle. Ricochet's head swivels like I've got him on a lead, and he comes trotting up to me. Ears pricked and tail high, like he's just as glad to see me as I am to see him. His coat is warm and silky under my hands.

"How did you do that?" Astrid is standing in the door-way, mystified. "Are you some kind of horse genius?"

"No." I can't stop smiling. Astrid called me a horse genius. "But Ricochet and I go way back."

"Look at him!" She shuffles a bridle, trying to put it in order. "What a beauty he is! And clearly smart, if you've taught him to come at the whistle. Is this the horse you're saving for?"

"How—how'd you know?"

"Simple. Why else would you teach him tricks?" She shrugs and disappears into the stable before I can tell her that's not what I meant.

I meant *how did you know I was saving for a horse?*

Soon enough, Ricochet is tacked up and I'm on his back and I take a long moment, there in the horseway, to sit with the flood of joy that comes with riding this horse whom I love that's almost, almost mine.

I'm not worried that Ricochet will spook on the trail. Fleet trainers lead mares along paths in the greenwood with their foals trailing along so the babies get used to the sound of squirrels chattering and birds rattling the branches. As they grow up, the colts and fillies won't be scared when things crash or chirr, or when their hooves clack against rocks.

They'll be sure-footed and steel-hearted if they and their riders ever happen upon bandits.

We wander at a lovely walk along the paths, around trees, past boulders, uphill, and across the meadow.

Astrid finds a new half-trail that none of us have ever seen, one that's thick with brush and morning glory, but it's more exciting than scary. When I'm with Ricochet, I can do anything.

Ricochet is eager. He'd like to go faster, but I keep him to a walk. He'll be back at the royal stables by suppertime, and I want to make every moment count.

"Not for long, though," I murmur, patting his neck. "Only a few more months. Then you'll live here. There's got to be room, and it can't cost much. We'll ride this trail every day. You and me."

Just the thought makes me smile. How possible it suddenly feels. Possible is not something you're used to in the lanes.

When we get back to the outrider stable, Jubilee is gone. I smile bigger as I untack Ricochet, give him a quick grooming, and turn him out. The doctor must have come by, just like Lucan said, and now she'll be fine.

Supper is grilled sausages, and I pile three on my plate along with a heap of fried potatoes and a handful of carrot sticks. When I get to our table, there's a boy I don't recognize sitting between Ivar and Ravik. His head is shaved and there's a gold ring in his ear, and his plate is barely visible under a mountain of food.

"Ah. Hello." I take a seat across from him, but he only half-glances at me while chewing.

"This is Gowan," Astrid says from the other end of the table. "He's joining the cadre."

"In case you don't stick around," Ivar adds, and when he smiles, I know for a fact he's running a pay table on it.

"Why wouldn't I stick around?" I ask coldly.

Ivar gives me a pointed *you know why* look, and I fight a scowl.

"Well. How can he be in the cadre already?" I stab some potatoes. "There's no way he could have taken the test."

Ivar shrugs. "Some guys you just trust."

My hand freezes with my fork halfway to my mouth. Because when Ivar says *guys*, he doesn't just mean boys. He means boys from caretaker families who bring their laundry to the sweatshop where my mother works.

I slam down the fork, get up, step over the bench, and head out the door.

The sky is glowing, a thousand shades of every color from red to orange to deep, rich purple. Everything smells sweet and summery, fresh straw, new flowers, honey. I plow down the horseway and I don't stop till I'm at the outrider pasture. Ricochet is there, already part of the herd, grazing.

I press my forehead against the top fence rail. Just being near him makes me feel better, and right now I need all the feeling better I can get.

"Sonnia?"

Astrid. Standing behind me in a cute pink tunic and trousers. Give her a ribbony headband and she'd fit right in at a townhouse garden party.

"Don't listen to that bonehead," she says. "Gowan's all right. I know him from home. Come back and eat with us."

I snort-laugh. "Why? I'm not one of the *guys*."

"Neither am I."

"Of course you are!" I tweak a fold of her tunic. "In all the ways that matter, at least."

"Maybe," Astrid says, "but I earned it."

"*Earned* it?" I growl. "Help me understand how you earned being born in a caretaker family."

She laughs. She *laughs,* and I grit my teeth because I have to let kids like her laugh at me if I want to stay.

Finally she says, "I shouldn't have to explain it to you. How lane kids must earn everything twice."

"But you're not—"

"Scow End," Astrid cuts in. "By the public rubbish pile."

I snap my mouth shut. The red jacket. The nice boots. The pink tunic and cute haircut. That forthright, fleet-footed confidence.

I was so sure.

Finally I manage, "I-I won't say anything to the others."

"Sonnia." Astrid waits till I look at her. "We're all from the lanes. Lucan. Marcel. Gowan. Every kid in the cadre."

"Oh," I breathe, and it feels like all the air leaves my body because if they're not from caretaker families, maybe the rules really are different here. Maybe one day, I could be like them in all the ways that matter.

Only if I stay, though.

It works so much better when everyone's in.

I thought Deirdre chose me special. That I turned up at the track and she remembered the sticky little kid she used to watch.

"That's your horse, right?" Astrid gestures to Ricochet, obviously changing the subject, and I can't help but smile, the way she says *your horse* like it's already a done deal but also how she understands that neither of us really wants to talk about Ivar, or what he said about me staying, or how she came by enough dinars for that red jacket, or how she was the one to follow me out here.

Ricochet flicks his tail again. Tomorrow I'll come for morning chores and he'll likely be gone. The outrider stablemaster must know by now there's a stray in his pasture, and when Perihelion's trainer calms down, he'll explain and they'll call a boy to ride Ricochet back to the royal stables.

I'll say goodbye now. I'll stuff Ricochet full of treats and brush him and tell him how beautiful he is so I don't have to think about anything harder.

I put two fingers to my lips and whistle. Ricochet raises his head, then turns and comes toward me, first at a trot and then a canter. When he arrives at the fence, I climb up enough to run my hands over his shiny chestnut back. He turns an ear toward me, which is his way of giving me a hug.

Astrid elbows me and points up the horseway. The track stablemaster is approaching on a big spotted gelding. Perihelion's head trainer is with him, and to my surprise, so is Deirdre.

I jump off the fence and back away a few paces. Ricochet is in enough trouble without me adding to it.

"That him?" The track stablemaster gestures to Ricochet. I frantically try to catch Deirdre's eye, but she's careful to keep her brown pony in line with the others.

"He's the one," the trainer growls. "After what happened with Perihelion, he ought to be made into dog food."

White on his forehead, white on his feet.

The track stablemaster turns to Deirdre. "You want this horse to stay?"

She puts a hand to her chin like she's thinking it over. Then she glances at me and says, "Yeah, he'll make a good outrider. No need to bother the royal stables."

Perihelion's trainer starts to bluster, but the track stablemaster asks to have a look at the big gold stallion, so the three of them ride on, up the horseway toward the huge fancy barns.

"What just happened?" I breathe, but Astrid grins and bumps my shoulder.

"That's great news for you!" she says. "Runcible gets to stay here!"

"Ricochet," I reply, and then it hits me that she's right and I scramble over the fence to hug him around the neck.

"You're staying!" I squeal into his mane. I kneel and press a hand over the hoof that's mine, then gently run my hand upward over the foreleg that I'll soon have the coppers for. "We'll go riding every day. We'll get to know that trail—"

The trail.

If Ricochet is an outrider horse, it won't be long before one of the junior racing cadre takes him on the Night Ride.

Flying headlong through the greenwood in the dark, with only the moon to guide his footfalls, urged on by a kid who only thinks to put dinars in their pocket.

I press against Ricochet, and my twenty-two coppers feel lighter than ever.

8

THE STABLEHANDS HAVE no idea why Deirdre might ride with the track stablemaster. They shrug it off like it's no big deal, how he not only asked for her opinion on whether Ricochet should stay, but he also overruled the trainer of the king's prize stallion and told him to walk on like he might to an old cart horse.

The kids are more interested in what kind of pie there'll be for dessert. Especially Gowan, who barely talks but eats his body weight in whatever's put in front of him.

After morning chores, I go looking for Deirdre. She thought she was doing a kind thing, keeping Ricochet here for me, but she has to help me get him back to the royal stables.

The first place I check is the racetrack, but it's quiet except for the draft horses pulling the giant metal contraption that rakes the dirt even. A horseboy tells me there'll be breezing runs later, so I wander the complex while I wait, hoping to bump into her. I walk past receiving barns and troughs and a little window with a small grill of metal bars that must be the betting office.

Next to the barred window is a big board with a wooden frame. There are six slots running down the edge, each with the name of a racehorse painted on a thin piece of wood and slid inside a metal holder. Perihelion, Maximiliana, Ishtar. Beside the horses are six more slots, which must be the names of jockeys because they're things like Benno and Felix and Simon. The rest of the board is painted black and covered with numbers chalked in a grid, which I'm not sure what to make of.

I'm not the best at school, but I can tell that none of the jockey names are *Deirdre*.

When the racehorses finally turn up, the jockeys are close behind, but Deirdre isn't among them.

I check all the racehorse barns and even try the jockey house, where the lot of them live, but the man who answers the door says she isn't there.

"I'm kind of worried," I tell Paolo as I watch him fill hay nets in the storage shed. "What if she got dismissed the same way Ricochet did? What if the track stablemaster blamed her for Perihelion losing and got rid of her?"

"Nah," Paolo replies. "Doesn't work that way. Sure, Deirdre blew her big chance to impress the king and win a share of a fat purse. It was beyond humiliating, so she's probably sulking somewhere. She definitely won't ride in the next race, and possibly the one after that. But the track stablemaster likes her. He's not turning her out anytime soon."

"He—ohhh." That would explain a lot. Why they were riding together. Why the track stablemaster would ask her opinion, why he'd ignore Perihelion's trainer, and why the stablehands wouldn't think anything of it.

In my mind, Deirdre is still a kid, older than me but too young for things like courting. But it's been a long time. She's grown up enough for a sweetheart.

Although the track stablemaster has the years to be her father, which is more than a little weird.

One morning after breakfast, the kids don't head for the field with their ball or toward the bunkhouse with their books. Instead we gather in the horseway, and Lucan is grinning when he tells me, "It's payday. The *best* day!"

For once, I don't mind giving up time with Ricochet. Today I'll finally be able to keep my promise to send money home *and* I'll own one of his forelegs, unlucky white markings and all.

We don't head toward the track's main office near the entry gate. We don't go to the betting window where there must be a cash box. Instead, we end up in a dim stable tucked behind the compost heap at the far end of the horseway. The stalls are clean but empty. The other kids fold into a line against the wall in front of a little red door next to a chalkboard covered with feeding instructions. I join them, baffled.

Ravik is first, and he opens the door and steps up what must be a staircase.

Ahead of me in line, Astrid and Julian are talking about the Night Ride. Julian is frustrated that he can never seem to finish higher than fifth.

"You ride timid," Astrid tells him. "You can't be afraid. Fear makes you doubt yourself, and that means your horse will too."

"Benno said that as well," Julian murmurs. "He said I'd be out of the cadre if I can't make the pay table interesting."

Astrid snorts. "You know Benno can't just decide that, right? He's a greedy jerk, and he's trying to scare you."

"It's working!" Julian's voice warps. "I can't get kicked out. I just can't."

Father sounds scared like that when he and Mother are short on the rent. They agonize over what to pawn—Grandma's locket? Our winter quilts?—or we go without food for as long as it takes, because the landlord will not hesitate to turn us all out on the street if we're even a day late with the coppers we owe.

Marcel sounded excited for the Night Ride. Ivar jangled his winnings at me.

It never occurred to me that the kids may only be doing it because they have no choice.

"That's got to be why Gowan's here," Julian whispers. "Benno doesn't make threats."

Astrid puts a comforting hand on Julian's shoulder. "Trust me. You're not why Gowan's here."

She cuts the smallest glance at me and my throat goes tight.

"Maybe you should pick a different horse," Astrid goes on. "Maybe that would help."

Not Ricochet. Choose him and I'll—

I'll what? I scuff my heavy work boots against the concrete floor. Beat Julian up? That might work once, but it would make Deirdre look bad and I'd be dismissed from the cadre and there'd be no one to protect Ricochet from the Night Ride.

"No one will choose him," I whisper. "He doesn't know the trail."

Yet.

One by one, kids come down the stairs and drift out the stable door. They all look happy, even Gowan, who hasn't worked long enough to earn much pay. Since I'm last in line, I'm alone in the stable when Ivar goes upstairs. When he returns, he smiles at me, slow and sly as if he knows something I don't.

I ignore him and climb the narrow, rickety staircase. It's dim and steep, the steps noisy like chickens an hour past their feeding time. At the top, there's a tiny landing, barely big enough to balance on, and a curtain made from feed sacks stitched together with hay twine.

I tap the doorframe and say, "Hello?"

"Come in."

I was expecting a beaky-nose underling from the purser's office, or maybe the outrider stablemaster. Not the girl who threaded ribbons through tiny Greta's toes to keep her busy while she showed Torsten and me how to peel an apple in one long continuous delicious strand.

When I push the curtain back, Deirdre is perched on a fruit crate with a metal strongbox on her knees. She's wearing riding clothes, and her hair is braided back tight, like she's about to put a helmet over it.

I think my mouth is frozen open.

Deirdre smiles. "You're still here. I like being right."

Everything about her is approving. It warms me like a coverlet made of afternoon sun.

The room is barely big enough to turn around in. There's a window cut into the wall, but no frame or glass in it. The saw marks are still on the wood, and it's not anything near a perfect square. There's a pile of blankets, an apple crate, and something that once may have been a chair.

"I knew you were a good bet." Deirdre flips open the cash box and gestures for me to hold out my hands. There's the soft, musical *plink* of coins and her fingers are warm where they brush mine, but when she pulls away, there's a bronze half-dinar coin and a scattering of coppers.

Greta's always teasing me about my figuring, but

even I can count, and this is not what I was promised.

"So . . ." I'm trying to find a way to say this nice. "You told me that I'd earn three hundred coppers a month."

"I also told you it would cost to stay here."

My stomach drops. I poke through the coins in my hand, but they are blurry and there's too much figuring.

She *did* tell me it would cost, but if I'm honest, that part galloped right past because all I could think about was Ricochet.

Deirdre puts aside the strongbox and stands up. At first I think she's going to hug me, but she gets right in my face and growls, "You have your own room. Dry. Comfortable. With a lock on the door. Yes?"

It stops me. I never once worried about the door to my house. My father was there, and Torsten.

Unless that's not the door she means.

"Yes, but—"

"Good food, as much as you want, three times a day. Second helpings. *Thirds.* Meat at every meal. Fruit and vegetables. Not squishy or rotten, either." Deirdre folds her arms. "And you're complaining."

"You told me I'd get three hundred coppers a month. Bed and board can't cost so much that this is what's left."

"You're mad about the *money*?" She puts a hand to her forehead, then whips it away quickly. Her face is a mask. "You know what? You should go home, then."

"No." It comes out panicky. "Please. I can't."

"It's not like you're forced to be here. This isn't royal service, and it's not a hiring fair contract. I thought you came because you wanted that horse."

I came because of Ricochet. I *stayed* because I can't imagine any other job but taking care of horses.

"But I made a mistake," Deirdre goes on. "I shouldn't have fought so hard to get you a position. I shouldn't have promised the track stablemaster that you were going to stick it out. I'm sorry. It was mean of me."

I study my feet, my belly full of hot worms. She's done so much for me already, and this makes her look bad.

"I thought you were ready to fight for what you wanted—no, not wanted, *deserved*—regardless of what anyone said. That we had that in common, you and I." Deirdre shakes her head, slow and disappointed. "It's a shame, because that horse you love? He clearly loves you. But you do what you need to do."

I look down at the coins in my hand. It seems like a lot until I consider how Father hands over five times as much to the shadowy, moustached creep that the landlord sends to collect the rent. I've seen Mother count out half as much to the butcher for our meat for a week. The ponies need hay and we need shoes and there's always something wrong with the roof—

He's not a want.

"I'm staying." I grip the coins tighter. "I told you I'd be the best stablehand, and I will be."

Deirdre considers me, like just maybe I measure up. "I hope so."

I wait, hoping she'll say something else. That she wishes things were different. Even that she's sorry.

Instead she glances pointedly at the doorway, and I take the hint.

There's a pile of straw bales in the corner of the stable, and when I get downstairs, I collapse onto one. My hand stings from clutching the coins so hard, and I open my fist slowly, hoping I was wrong somehow. That a few of the coins that looked like coppers are really half-dinars, and there's more money here than I thought.

In my palm are a single bronze half-dinar coin and—I count carefully, twice—thirty coppers. There are a hundred coppers in a dinar, so that means half of a hundred is . . .

Not enough.

Even if I send home every copper, it still won't make up the difference.

Behind me, the door to the staircase squeaks, and I turn in time to see Paolo pulling it open and stepping inside. He must not have seen me tucked away back here, so I settle into the straw bale, tip my head back, and swallow down tears.

It must be payday for companion horse keepers, too, and when Paolo comes down, I'll wave him over and he'll make a joke about light pockets and we'll laugh and I'll feel better for a moment or two, before I have to think of what I'm going to tell Father.

I jingle the coins in my hand. Part of me wants to throw them across the room, but instead I dig an empty drawstring bag out of the cleaning cupboard. At one time it had soap flakes in it, but I dump out the last of them, slide in the coins, and cinch the string closed.

These don't belong with my pony ride coppers. I wasn't allowed to keep every coin that Hazy and Boris and Buttermilk earned, but at least Father was honest about how many I'd get.

Footsteps echo and squeal on the stairs, and Paolo's voice is suddenly distinct. "Look, they know you're here, and yes, you're right—I'm supposed to find out why, but I'm also supposed to tell you it's okay for you to come home."

I go still. If I move now, Deirdre and Paolo will hear me. They'll think I'm eavesdropping on purpose.

Deirdre snorts. "Should be pretty clear why. Even to them."

"They miss you. Even with you leaving like you did."

"Tell them whatever you want. It won't change anything. I'm staying. There's more dinars in a pay table."

Paolo laughs. "I told them you'd say something like that."

I stay frozen as he reaches the bottom of the stairs and breezes out of the stable. Deirdre is behind him. She leans out the entrance and glances both ways, quick, cautious. Then she kneels beside a wooden feed chest. She puts the cash box inside and locks the chest with a key on a long string around her neck, then disappears into the horseway.

They probably tell you it's foolish, right? Wanting something so big? So unimaginable?

Deirdre's family must not want her to be a jockey. Maybe they're the sort of people who think it's a man's job, or they're worried for her safety.

I sit for a long moment, waiting for her to be absolutely gone, and to distract myself, I try hard to remember Paolo from when I was small. He and Deirdre clearly know each other, and have for some time. Maybe she brought him with her sometimes when she watched us. A cousin, maybe, or a neighbor.

In a while, the stable is quiet, and so is the horseway outside. I tuck the soap flake bag into my barn jacket alongside my pony ride coppers and head to the outrider stable. It's midmorning, free time, so I grab a grooming box and call Ricochet from the pasture with our whistle. I crosstie him outside, under the covered overhang, and pick up the stiff bristle brush.

Flick. Flick. Flick. I whip the bristles up and away from Ricochet's coat so the dirt flies behind it. Just like Father showed me when I had to reach up to curry Buttermilk.

They'll go hungry. That'll be the first thing. Mother and Father, then Greta.

"Sonnia?" Lucan stands a generous horselength away, holding Hollyhock by the halter. "We're getting ready to—are you crying?"

Having an older brother means you know the answer to this question is always *no* and sometimes *shove off, of course not.* But right now I don't care what anyone thinks of me.

"It's just . . . I have to send coppers home to help my family, but I hoped to save some, too." I scrub my eyes with my wrist. "It's not enough, though. What I got today. Not even to make the rent."

Lucan doesn't reply, and he's like Mother or Father in that moment. There's something he means but doesn't want to say.

"No." I face him, gripping the brush like a club. "I won't join the Night Ride. I refuse to have anything to do with it."

If things get really bad, one of the ponies will have to go, and it will be Buttermilk. She's old, older than me, and she needs medicines and expensive special mashes that Hazy and Boris don't.

"Hey, maybe this will help." Lucan fishes through his pockets and pulls out a cylinder wrapped in brown paper. He snaps it in half and hands a section to me.

A series of metal circlets tumble from the broken paper into my palm. Toll road tokens. Lucan has a whole *roll* of them.

"They're just sitting in my pocket. I keep getting

them, and there's no way I'll ever use them all." He glances at me sidelong. "You won't be the only one who sends coppers home."

I poke the tokens back into the paper roll as the world expands again and again. If I can use the toll roads, it won't take most of a day to get to Edge Lane and back.

I can visit home. I can see my family.

It's a gift out of nowhere. A gift of the possible.

"Thank you. It helps a lot, actually." Not as much as it could, but it's more than I had a few moments ago. I manage half a laugh. "Maybe I should try selling them to the other stablehands to make up the difference. Looks like I won't be getting to five hundred coppers any other way."

"Won't work. Everyone's got their own tokens."

I open my mouth to ask why I'm not included in *everyone*, but I see it in his face. If the Night Ride has a pay table and a five-dinar purse for the winner every time, there's someone with deep pockets making a fortune on the wagering. Probably many someones, noblemen and the townhouse wealthy who love dinars more than they fear the king, and way more than they care about the well-being of stablehands and outrider horses.

The kids who go along, even half willingly, have their feed bins topped up with grain and treats.

The rest of us stand on our cracked hooves.

"Five hundred coppers, eh?" Lucan forces a smile.

"Please tell me you're saving for a pair of decent boots. Those belong on the scrap heap."

"Just as soon as I buy this gorgeous boy right here," I reply, and I pat Ricochet's gleaming chestnut shoulder lovingly.

Lucan frowns. "What? That can't be right. This horse has to be worth more than five dinars."

"No, he costs fifty." I smooth a section of Ricochet's mane. "The royal stablemaster told me so."

"Then you're going to need way more than five hundred coppers."

"No, I did the figuring," I tell him, but a cold, sinking feeling is spreading through my insides. I did it on my own, without thinking to ask Greta. When the idea of owning Ricochet was so far away and impossible that I didn't want anyone making fun of how silly it sounded.

"I hate to tell you this," Lucan says slowly, "but fifty dinars isn't five hundred coppers. It's five *thousand*."

Ricochet shifts his weight and takes a mouthful of hay. The sound of him chewing fills the silence.

Five thousand coppers.

I could give pony rides until my hair goes gray. I could go to the hiring fairs and take contract after contract.

There is no way on this green earth that I can ever in my life earn five thousand coppers.

Master Harold must have known. All this time he smiled into my face and politely asked how my saving was going, always well aware that Ricochet would live a nice long life and find his way to the big paddock in the sky long before I had anything close to coppers enough to buy him.

"Sonnia?" Lucan shifts awkwardly. "You all right?"

"No," I whisper, and I lower my forehead onto Ricochet's warm back and fight tears with everything I have.

Master Harold could have simply told me. Instead I've spent all this time believing Ricochet was within my grasp. That all I had to do was work hard and scrape my coppers into a pile, that the king valued Ricochet as a fleet horse and wouldn't sell him to anyone but me.

Instead Master Harold said nothing. Like Deirdre. They both said nothing and let me make a fool of myself.

"You keep saying you're here to stay." Lucan's voice is gentle. "Maybe you should give the Night Ride a chance."

I don't reply. Tears are slipping out and sliding into Ricochet's silky back. I've done all these things for him, to be near him, to make it so we could always be together, and now he's further away than he's ever been.

9

TWO BARNS DOWN from Perihelion's, I find Deirdre trying to sweet-talk the head trainer of a glorious bay named Hesperides into choosing her to ride him in the next race.

"I know Benno posted better times this week," Deirdre is saying, "but my times were better than his last week, and no one can get a horse to come from behind like I can. Hesperides is not going to set the pace with that prince's chestnut filly, and you know it."

"Ehhh, I'll think about it." The trainer is a graybeard, scruffy and round, with the kind of weathered face that's seen generations of horses win and place and show. Not the sort of face that's easily flattered and persuaded, and Deirdre's big-eyed sugar-bomb smile doesn't last once she turns away.

It goes smooth as granite when she sees me coming. "If this is about your wages, there's nothing—"

"No. Not that." I glance at Hesperides' trainer, directing a handful of grooms and someone who must be his exercise rider. "I need help. There's no one else I can ask. Please."

Deirdre steers me into a narrow gap between two racehorse barns. It's pleasantly cool here, a refreshing pour of shade, and her face is carefully blank, like the yard just after it snows.

I pull in a long, shaky breath. "I know the track stablemaster has a crush on you. Can you get him to send Ricochet back to the royal stables?"

"He *what*? Eew. No! Why would you think that?" Deirdre laughs and makes a show of shuddering. "Definitely not. On both counts. Ricochet's staying here."

"But why?" I keep my voice calm. "However he feels about you, the track stablemaster listens to you. I know you kept Ricochet here as a favor to me, but he needs to go back. Today, if possible."

"I didn't—" She breaks off, peering at me. Then she says, "The track stablemaster listens to me because I'm one of the king's jockeys. We have many interests in common. Well, one interest: dinars. When I win, he wins."

"Please," I whisper. "If Ricochet's not at the royal stables, he won't be safe."

"What do you mean?" She leans closer. "He can't go back there. Why wouldn't he be safe at the track?"

The dark horseway lit silver. Kids on horseback disappearing into the night with dinars on their minds.

Jubilee with her hoof in the air, huddled in the shelter till I noticed her.

"Hey. Whatever it is, you can tell me." Deirdre's voice is warm and reassuring, nothing like the sharp stabbiness of the Deirdre with the strongbox from earlier, and all at once it's like I'm five again and I dropped my honey-on-a-spoon and she's going to fix it for me.

So I tell her everything I know about the Night Ride.

As I speak, Deirdre's arm tightens over my shoulder till I'm snugged against her, and all I can think is how long it's been since I've seen Mother, since she's given me a hug before I climbed into the loft to go to bed.

"The track stablemaster listens to you," I remind Deirdre. "If he knew about the Night Ride, he'd put a stop to it right away."

"Perhaps," she replies, "but then he'd want to know how I knew, and I'd have to tell him the truth—that you told me. He'd call you in and demand the whole story. If even half of what you said is happening, he'd have no choice but to turn all the stablehands over to the king. If he didn't and the king found out somehow, he'd be branded and exiled too. Horse harm is horse harm."

"But someone must be forcing the kids to do the Night Ride!" I insist. "How is it their fault if they have no choice?"

"The track stablemaster would likely turn you over to the king as well," Deirdre goes on. "He might not believe that you had nothing to do with it. Or he wouldn't want to take the chance."

I shudder, but still I whisper, "I have to protect Ricochet, though. I won't see him hurt. Whatever it costs."

"What does that mean?"

"I don't know. There has to be a way to stop the Night Ride without anyone getting in trouble." I make a helpless gesture. "There could be extra security, maybe. If grooms stand in the horseway with safety lamps, no one's going near the outriders. Maybe Master Harold at the royal stables could help. He loves Ricochet too, and he and my father have been friends a long time."

Deirdre's jaw works. She hasn't taken her eyes off me once, and it's a little unnerving. "I see. Well. There'll be real trouble for all of us if the king so much as suspects. So leave this with me. Like you said, people listen to me. I'll take care of everything. Okay?"

All at once I can pull in a whole breath, down to the bottom of my belly, and let out every terrifying thought that's been gathering there. Deirdre is going to fix this for me. For all of us.

"But that means you can't tell anyone else," she goes on. "There'd be a big reward for this information, and whoever you tell might go straight to the king. Then there's nothing I can do for Ricochet, or you, or any of my stablehands."

"No. I won't tell anyone." I shake my head like that will prove it.

Leave this with me. I'll take care of everything.

It's like being tucked into bed or handed a steaming mug of tea on a freezing winter day. I pull the warmth of it around me like a blanket, as tight as a hug.

The other kids are already cleaning the outrider pasture when I arrive, and as I watch Ivar pretend to stab Julian in the rear with a pitchfork, it occurs to me that Deirdre called them *my stablehands*, as if she'd bought their labor at the hiring fair.

It's been three days since I was paid. My soap flake bag sits untouched in my apple crate.

I can't keep putting it off. Even if it's not enough, something is better than nothing. So one afternoon, once the horses are put up after the trail ride, I palm some of Lucan's toll road tokens and head home.

The cobbles are smooth and perfect under my big clunky boots, and passing the tollbooths makes me think of the coins in my pocket, how the right thing to do is give them all to Mother and Father and smile big like I'm happy about it.

I try to do some figuring. Half of eighty is . . . still not enough.

As I get near the house, my footsteps slow. The coins get heavier, and I seriously consider tossing the soap flake bag through the window and running away hard.

I can't, though. I miss my family. If I wanted to avoid

them, I'd have come in the morning when they were all at work or school.

I just wish I could be sure they'd understand.

When I hear Boris and Hazy and Buttermilk out back, I duck into the rear yard to say hello to them first. They nicker and whuffle when I poke my head into the stable, and they crowd to the half doors like they've missed me.

I pet Boris's neck and scratch Hazy's forehead and run a corncob along Buttermilk's back. It's cozy, and I pull up a bucket and sit with them, petting and fussing.

A shadow falls across the doorway and Father appears holding a cudgel. When he sees it's me, he drops it and flings his arms wide. "Sonnia!"

I'm up the short aisle in three steps and holding him tight. His leather coat is smooth and stiff and smells like sheep grease and I am *home*.

"I thought you were a bandit!" he says with a straggly laugh. "It's so good to see you. Greta will be especially happy. She can't wait to go back to school."

"But why hasn't—" I turn it into a cough. I know very well why. Since I'm not here to give pony rides, Greta has had to take my turns as well as hers.

In that moment, I know I have no choice but to give my family every copper.

I follow Father into the house. He stands near the doorway, too polite to ask outright, and my face feels hot as I put the soap flake bag on the table and step back, away from the soft, empty way the cloth folds over itself.

Father reaches for the bag and his hand comes up fast, like he expected it to be heavier. I want to tell him, but I don't know how to explain without feeling like an absolute fool who agreed to something without learning the full terms of it.

Greta pushes the door open with her backside while swinging in a full bucket of water. When she sees me, she grins and squeals, "You're here! Did you bring coppers? Like you promised?"

It hits like a cold spike of wind, but I manage a smile and reply in my best teasing voice, "Hello to you, too. I'm well. Thank you for asking."

Father has poured the coins into his hand. They fit in one big, work-roughened palm. I try to catch his gaze, but he's not looking up.

Greta lowers the bucket by the fire and bounces over. "Let me see. They wouldn't have given you a hundred and fifty individual coppers. Or maybe they would. It's not like you're good at counting."

She says it playfully, teasing back, but I know exactly what Father has in his hand, and it's not what any of them are expecting.

One glance at the coins, though, and Greta's eyes come up incredulous. "This is all you're giving us? What happened to a hundred and fifty coppers?"

"It's all I have!" I protest. "I had to pay for room and board."

"Sure it is," she mutters, "after you made sure you kept enough for a fetlock. Or do you have enough for a shin now?"

"It's not like that!"

Greta sighs and shakes her head, then trudges to the bench by the fire where she sits with her back to me and doesn't reach for a book. Usually she's reading something thick and heavy that she borrowed from Mistress Crumb, but the little shelf where she keeps books safe is empty.

"Is it true?" Father asks me. "Is this really all the money you earned? You didn't keep some back for Ricochet?"

"Yes! It's every last copper they gave me. I swear!"

Father tips his big hand so the coins clink. "I'll have to speak with your mother, then. I don't see how this can continue."

"What?" I gasp. "Father. No. I can't quit. I *won't*."

"We agreed you'd send home enough coppers to cover your share of pony rides. It's not fair to expect your sister to do all the work while you spend time with Ricochet."

"But that's not—how can you—" I lift my chin. "You expect me and Greta to help out, but Torsten got to leave. How is that fair?"

"Your brother received an invitation to royal service," Father replies, and there's a note of warning in his voice. "Torsten isn't just a stablehand. He's a stablehand for the king of Mael Dunn."

Father doesn't mean it to sting. It does, though. Both of us know Master Harold had one big ask, and he's known my brother and sister and me our whole lives. Master Harold knows Greta loves books and Torsten loves solving puzzles, and I'm the one who wants nothing more than to spend every moment of every day with horses—riding them, currying them, even shoveling up after them.

He knows Greta should be a teacher and Torsten should be a magistrate, and *I'm* the one who belongs in a stable.

Master Harold had one big ask, and there's no reason he couldn't have asked for me.

Except for all the reasons he couldn't ask for me.

"I'm not *just* a stablehand either." I watch my coins disappear into my father's pocket, and what comes out of my mouth is "I've been invited to join the junior racing cadre and learn to ride racehorses for the king."

Greta turns, hooking an elbow over the back of the bench. She seems interested in spite of herself. "You're kidding. Really? You're going to be the next girl jockey? So they've got you doing schooling races?"

I must look as confused as I feel, because she goes on, "That's when you ride a real racehorse on a real track, with trainers watching to judge your form and give you pointers."

"Well, no, but . . ." I stop because I sound clueless. I have no idea what jockey training would look like because the junior racing cadre spends more time on trail rides and cleaning leather than it does anywhere near the track.

"Surely they're at least showing you how to sit a racing saddle?" Greta sounds excited now. "How to balance? How to change leads around a turn?"

"What do you know about it?" I snap.

"I read *books* now and then?"

Greta rolls her eyes like it's obvious and turns back toward the fire, but my heart is skidding all over the place because, as usual, she's right. If the junior racing cadre is supposedly learning to ride racehorses for the king, there's only so much they're going to gain from trail rides.

"Your mother will be home soon," Father says. "We'll discuss this over supper."

He says it like the matter is closed, and I have the sudden, certain feeling that Mother will agree that I should come home and go back to giving pony rides. Walking in a circle, going nowhere, leading ponies while other kids ride.

I edge toward the door. "You know what? I need to go. It'll be time for evening chores soon. I love you both, and Mother, too, and I'll send more coppers when I have them. Bye."

"Sonnia. Don't you dare walk away from—"

But I'm in the lane, then around the corner, fumbling for a toll road token, moving from a trot to a canter when I hear Greta yelling my name. I mutter a curse, but I slow to a walk so she can catch up.

"Wait." She's panting. She does more reading than running. "Father's right. It's not fair."

My sister's nose is peeling. Her braid is falling apart, like it's been several days since she took it down and ran a brush through her hair.

"I can't just not show up for chores," I tell her. "People at the racetrack are counting on me. You know how horses are."

Greta's face goes hard. "Right. Ricochet. Precious, darling Ricochet. What could *possibly* be more important than him?"

"It's not that!" I can't look at her, though. "I made a promise."

"You made a promise to Mother and Father, too." She kicks at the mud. "You made a promise to me."

I keep walking. Fast, head down.

Greta trails to a stop. "Okay. I get it. You win."

She turns and heads home without looking back.

I'm left in the middle of the street with nothing I can say. No way to make it better, for Greta or for me.

Even though I have a whole pocketful of toll road tokens, I take the lanes back to the racetrack. They curve and twist and dead-end into one another, but while I'm walking through the guts of Mael Dunn, I'm not anywhere. Not home. Not at the track.

Somewhere I'm not disappointing anyone.

When I was small, I wanted so badly to be like Deirdre. She could reach high shelves and fix broken toys. She could persuade shopkeepers to give us palmfuls of cookie dust and bruised fruit. There was nothing she couldn't do.

They probably tell you it's foolish, right? Wanting something so big? So unimaginable?

No one has to tell me. I already know.

By the time I get back to the bunkhouse, I'm not upset anymore. Just the kind of bone-deep tired that whispers how giving up makes sense. At least pony rides are a sure thing. After a while I can buy some candy sticks. Maybe a decent pencil for school.

I hug Ricochet extra long at evening chores and go to bed early. I'm not even that tired. I'm just ready for today to end.

It's the blackest part of night when I blink awake to rapping on my door. Knuckles, fast and urgent.

Lucan. His outline is cut sharp from the moonlight streaming through the bunkhouse window.

"Ivar's saddling Ricochet," he says in a low voice, and he's back up the hallway and out the door before I fully reckon it.

It's the middle of the night. If Ivar is planning to ride Ricochet, there's only one reason for it.

10

I CATCH UP to Lucan in heartbeats, then pass him. I'm running full out, and each step I take fills me with more rage.

A mounted shadow crosses the horseway, its hooves muffled by dirt. It's moving with intent toward the field where the trailhead is. There's a few more shadows near the outrider stable. Marcel. Astrid. Gowan. Bertram.

But I pass them all and head straight for Ivar.

Sure enough, Ricochet is crosstied in the aisle and Ivar is tightening the saddle girth. He's dressed in black riding silks and seems made of darkness. Ricochet nickers when he sees me, and I force myself into something like a state of calm. Horses can tell when people are upset and they'll act accordingly.

"Put my horse away," I say to Ivar in a low, even voice that's much less violent than I feel.

"*Your* horse?" Ivar smirks as he tightens a strap. "Last

I heard, you were scrounging coppers still. So I'm riding him tonight."

He reaches for the bridle lying over a nearby half door, but I yank it away. The bit jangles against the rings and Ricochet tosses his head, grunting.

"No one's riding tonight," I growl.

"Sonnia." Lucan pauses in the doorway like he's worried something will explode. "The moon's up. The pay table is set. The Night Ride will be starting soon."

I glance at the horseway lit silver. Deirdre couldn't have misunderstood what needs to happen.

"People are coming right now to put a stop to this," I tell them. "If you don't want to be caught taking one of the king's horses without permission for an illegal, dangerous race, you may want to go back to the bunkhouse."

Ivar cackles. "Yeah, I doubt that." He steps around us and disappears into the tack room. He's going to get another bridle. One Ricochet won't be familiar with.

"You're not hearing me." Lucan steps closer. "The Night Ride is happening with you or without you."

I put a hand on Ricochet's side. His muscles are drawn and he's whuffling like he does when it's time to run. On the exercise course at the royal stables, there was a stretch where I'd give him his head and away he'd go, as fast as he wanted for as long as he wanted.

Ivar reappears with a bridle. Ricochet has only been on the trail a handful of times, and Ivar doesn't like to lose.

I can't wait for Deirdre.

Before Ivar can get near, I shake the bridle in my hands into shape, slide the bit into Ricochet's mouth, settle the straps, and swing onto his back. He dances into the horseway, tossing his head. Eager to go.

"Benno's always complaining that the pay table isn't interesting enough," Astrid says with a grin as she appears next to us on Mandalay. "You riding ought to make him happy."

"Isn't Benno a jockey?" I ask. "What can he—why—?"

"Come, I'll show you where we line up."

I can't do this. It's too dangerous.

"The rules are simple," Astrid says as we leave the horseway. "We line up in the field. Last Ride's winner drops a handkerchief. When it hits the ground, you go. Same trail we ride every day, so no surprises."

No wonder it's the exercise course for the outriders. So they get to know it in the daylight well enough to run it in the dark.

"There are flags at the first tight turn, the creek, the meadow, and the craggy rock." Astrid speaks quiet and calm, as if we weren't riding toward kids dressed in black in a shadowy line across the field, edged with silvery moonlight. "Every checkpoint has its own color. If you don't turn up with all four flags in the right colors, you're disqualified. No coppers. No nothing."

"What if the first kid takes all the flags?" I ask. "To keep everyone else from winning?"

"They won't. It'd be obvious at the finish line and the pay table would be messed up and that's bad for everyone. Especially the kid that did it."

I shudder. "Where's the finish line?"

"Back pasture. There'll be a chalk line at the end nearest the workhorse stable. Benno's there to call win, place, and show." She glances at me. "We walk the horses cool in the pasture before we put them away for the night."

There's that, at least. The horses won't go into their stalls wet and their health put at risk.

Astrid and I join the line of kids in the field. No one says anything. The horses whuffle and shift.

My belly is churning. I just won't go. Everyone else will leap forward and I'll stay behind. I'll walk Ricochet back to the stable and put him away.

Fifty coppers, though. Fifty coppers just for finishing.

There's a dulled canter behind me, and up comes Ivar on Banner. He pulls a white cloth from his jacket, holds it at arm's length, and lets it fall. It's halfway down before it occurs to me what it means—that the race is starting. I've barely had a chance to shift my weight and take a good grip on the reins when all the other horses in the line rush forward toward the dark mouth of the trailhead.

Ricochet is a whole heartbeat behind them, but he leaps like a burst dam, throwing us forward so hard that I almost fly off. I grip and scrabble for a handhold, gasping for breath. We're hurtling toward the trailhead and its eerie dark tunnel that leads straight into the greenwood and heavens only know what else.

No. I know everything that's there. I've ridden that trail every day for weeks now. The main trails and the offshoots. I know where it's wide and where it's narrow.

All I have to do is finish. Lucan said so. And I mean to finish at a sedate, careful walk, or perhaps a trot, but Ricochet has other ideas. He's among running horses and he's not listening to my repeated *whoa, boy*.

We pass Bertram on Pennant. Then Gowan, who was brought into the cadre solely because someone who matters was sure I wouldn't stay.

We're not last anymore. I grin hard in spite of myself. In spite of the fact that what I'm doing is dangerous and foolhardy.

The opening in the greenwood is only big enough for one horse at a time, and I squeeze my eyes shut as Ricochet flies through the gap—branches tearing at my hair and jacket—and onto the trail.

Ricochet gallops along the straight stretch that in daytime is a pleasant, shady path, and with the moon so bright, I start to get my bearings even through the greenwood's canopy. Astrid said the first checkpoint is the tight turn, which is after this stretch widens and past a series of blackberry brambles.

Hoofbeats drum behind us, and before I can respond, Ricochet speeds up. I lurch, then move with him, flattening myself over his neck. My eyes start to water from the speed as we fly past a dark horse-shaped blur that's moving at an uncertain lope.

I almost whisper *good boy* before I catch myself. Neither of us should be out here. None of this is good.

Except fifty coppers, which is *very* good.

The tight turn is just ahead, and two horses are paused in the bend. As we canter closer, I can see kids reaching up to loosen strips of cloth from a branch overhead. Whoever tied them knew that horses wouldn't like anything that flutters, and the strips are in tight bows.

Ricochet pushes between the riders like he's done this a million times, and I find myself next to Marcel and Ravik. Each of them works quick and intent, not bothering the other, but both horses are prancing and the boys have to untie their flags one-handed while they keep their mounts in place.

"Stand," I murmur to Ricochet, cueing him with my calves. Then I drop the reins, reach up, and untie a flag with both hands. I shove it in my barn jacket and urge Ricochet forward, leaving both Marcel and Ravik cursing behind me, still struggling to keep their horses steady.

The next part of the trail is uphill, and there are too many rocks for me to hurry Ricochet, so I give him his head and nudge him forward with my legs. "C'mon, c'mon, up you go, friend, as fast as you can."

His hooves hit rocks and make sickening *clodthuck*

sounds, but hooves are hard and they're made for this. The worst part is not being able to see any of it, but Ricochet's eyes are way better than mine.

Somehow we pass another dim horse-shaped shadow making its way uphill nearby. One of us isn't on the main trail, but it's too dark to know which and I doubt it matters. Astrid said we merely had to get a flag from each checkpoint, and the next one is the creek, which is at the bottom of the hill beyond the next straight stretch.

Two checkpoints means we're almost halfway done. No turned ankles. No broken legs. Only a little further and there'll be fifty coppers in my pocket.

The creek is about two lengths wide, but shallow, never higher than Ricochet's stockings. Two horses are balking hard on the gravel bank, and their riders are trying everything they can to urge them across. I guide Ricochet forward, untie another flag from an overhanging branch, and stuff it into my jacket. While I'm doing it, I can see why a horse might think the creek is dangerous—little silvery currents roll along the rocks like snakes and even the shallows seem bottomless.

But Ricochet is a fleet horse. He's seen water since he was small, probably at night as well as in the day, and he splashes across the creek like a champ.

The only problem is that the other two horses watch him do it, and they quickly work out that there's nothing to fear. They're behind us in no time, and now Ricochet is cantering and they're coming up fast behind him.

I start to rein him in, to let them pass, but Ricochet isn't having any of it. He puts on speed, hurtling through the dark toward the steep hill that ends in the meadow.

I pull in my knees and shift my weight, making myself small on his back. It's hard not to cheer him on as he keeps two riders behind us along a straightaway and then uphill.

To cheer *us* on.

The meadow is ghostly by moonlight, still crammed with flowers but silent except for the *shush-shush* of horses moving through tall grass. Three kids are leaning in their saddles to paw through a sprawling leafy shrub. I join them, pushing branches aside, peering for flags, before I notice a turn of cloth near the ground.

I'm out of the saddle in a heartbeat, telling Ricochet to stand. The other kids follow my lead, scrambling to dismount. Once a flag is in my jacket, I put one foot in the stirrup and cue Ricochet to go, landing in the saddle while the others are still trying to calm their horses enough to mount.

As we head into the trees, I count again. I think we're in the top three now. We're going to show.

Going downhill in the dark is beyond terrifying, but I give Ricochet his head once more. He knows what he's doing, and I trust him. I lean back in the saddle to help him balance his weight. His hooves clip and clop while unseen branches catch at my hair, but I pull in steady breaths and picture what the trail looks like in the daytime. Well-trodden. No rocks. No chuckholes.

I have to stay calm. If I'm not calm, Ricochet will know, and he'll panic. If he panics, we're both in trouble.

The greenwood is perfectly still. No birds. No creatures. The air smells damp and it's warmer than I'd have guessed, and moonlight silvers through the branches almost as bright as safety lamps.

It's beautiful in a way I never expected the night would be, not when Father and Mother always made us come in before dark. It's just me and Ricochet, and any time I spend with him is good time. And passing riders—

It's actually kind of fun.

It's not. It's *not.*

When we get to the bottom of the incline, the trail is flat for a good long way, and I tell Ricochet to gallop. The drum of it works into my legs and back like a kitten's purr, and wind curls around my face so fresh and brisk that I grin.

We emerge at the craggy rock. The final checkpoint. There's a series of bows tied along several nearby branches. A lot of them. Which means not many kids have passed here to take one.

There's a *crunch-crackle* behind us. Someone coming at a trot, and I don't stop to count bows. Ricochet stands while I untie a flag and stuff it into my barn jacket with the rest, and now we're home free. The back pasture is a gentle stretch of trail from here, and now I'm ahead of one more kid.

I cue Ricochet to gallop, and we're away.

He's not a racehorse. He never will be. But Ricochet loves to run, and I love riding him when he's doing something he loves. We fly through the night toward the back pasture. The gate is open, which is a major violation of track policy, and there's a horse-shaped shadow slowing down to negotiate its way through.

Fleet horses have been taught to move quick and steady past unusual obstacles and disregard flapping stirrups and dangling mailbags and get along with every kind of animal.

They've also been taught to jump.

We're in the air almost before I know it, and I can hardly breathe as we sail over the pasture fence and land—two hooves, four hooves—with a jolt that makes me slide hard in the saddle and grapple for a handhold.

As I recover, I spot Ivar coming through the gate. He's the shadow, and I'm close enough that I can see his mouth open like a fish for a long moment before he goes steely.

Ricochet has momentum from the gallop, and I guide him with a firm rein toward the end of the pasture where there's a dark pillar who must be Benno at the finish line. There are no horses in front of me. No obstacles.

"Go, friend," I whisper, and I give Ricochet his head once more because this pasture is safe and I want nothing more than for Ivar to eat dirt clods.

Behind us, there's a thundering of hooves as Ivar and

Banner try to catch up, but it's too late. Ricochet gallops past Benno, who holds up one arm as we fly by.

We made it. We're safe, both of us.

Ricochet needs to cool down, so I let him find his own pace along the pasture fence. When he drops into a walk, I slide down so we're shoulder to shoulder, and I lead him.

I can't stop petting his sweaty neck with hands that tremble. That ride was nothing like the exercise course at the royal stables.

There's a crowd of men gathered behind the finish line, just beyond the fence. There are at least a hundred, and they're blocking the gate.

Constables. They must be. They've come to arrest every one of us.

Something went wrong. Deirdre spoke with people she thought she could trust, but they had no reason to help her and every reason to turn us all in. They'd have gone straight to the track stablemaster, who called the law to save his own skin.

But the men don't pour into the field with billy clubs flying and handcuffs jingling. They seem to be lined up in front of a big trestle table and lurking near it. Waiting for something and willing to wait.

I recognize several of Perihelion's grooms. Hesperides' exercise rider is nearby, along with a handful of undertrainers. They're wearing hats pulled over their eyes and shabby barn jackets in dark colors.

"Rider." Benno gestures me over. He's got long hair that glints in the silver light and the swagger of a bandit king.

This can't be right. The jockeys can't be behind the Night Ride. They have the most of all to lose, and setting up a pay table would take dinars none of them have.

There's a bonus, too, if a horse wins with long odds. When the king wins big, he does not forget his jockeys.

When I edge near Benno, he says, "Flags?"

It takes a moment to remember what Astrid said about the flags, how you need four in the right colors or you're disqualified. I reach into my jacket, pull out the scraps of cloth, and lay them across Benno's palm. Ricochet behind me mouths his bit and shuffles.

Benno turns to the crowd behind him and lifts a single finger high in the air. "Sonnia. On . . . who is that? Ricochet?"

There's a groan so loud I cringe, waiting for the onrush of constables or even the track security guards who wander the grounds with cudgels to keep spectators polite.

There's also a single whoop of joy, followed by cackles and hoots of laughter and the *clinkety-clink* of metal on metal. Like coins being poured.

If jockeys are running the Night Ride, Deirdre would already know about it.

Unless they're cutting Deirdre out. The only girl jockey. The one who's close enough to the track stablemaster that he listens to her.

Benno turns the flags over, admiring. "You know how long it's been since we've had an upset? You're barely on the pay table, but anyone who put money down that you'd win is very happy right now." He smiles. "I happen to be one of them. And may I say it's about time you got with the program."

There are so many things *I* want to say. So many answers I want to demand. What comes out is "Wait. We won?"

Benno grins and hands me a drawstring pouch. It's heavy and it clanks. I loosen the cord and peek inside. There are five big gold coins. Five dinars.

The winner's purse.

The *program.*

Five dinars is a month's rent. It's food for a whole season. It's my share of pony ride money this month, and next month, and maybe more months after that.

It's Ricochet's whole leg. Or his wonderful, intelligent head with its unlucky white blaze.

"Go on now," Benno says to me, then he turns and gestures to Ivar, a dark blocky shape behind me. "Second-place rider. Flags."

The crowd of men has thinned enough that I can spot a table in its midst, and sure enough, there's someone behind it with a strongbox. A jockey—Felix, I think—is counting coins into a shadowy hand.

If I didn't know better, I'd say it was the same box that Deirdre had on payday.

Ricochet whuffles. He just ran a race. He needs water and a hot bran mash and a cozy stall to sleep in. I *clickclick* to him and lead him away, past the pay table. Something snares my sleeve and I startle, but it's only one of Perihelion's grooms. He's thin and pockmarked and grinning so big he looks ready to eat the world.

"Sorry. I just want to say thank you to this beautiful boy." The groom gently takes Ricochet's bridle and kisses him right on the nose. "I'm taking fifteen dinars home because of him! Oh, and you, too. For a wager of five coppers!"

"I—I thought the racetrack had a minimum bet," I stammer. "Fifty dinars, right? How could you wager five coppers?"

The groom lifts his brows. "Do you see anyone near the track betting window?"

"But why . . . why would you . . . ?"

I don't mean it as a real question, but he replies, "Mostly because of Ricochet. To annoy my boss. Perihelion's head trainer, I mean. You were barely on the pay table. A girl. Someone who'd never won a Night Ride. Someone who'd never even *ridden*, and Ricochet hardly knows the trail."

"I made the pay table interesting," I whisper.

"You shattered it, is what you did." The groom grins at me in wonderment. "How did you get him to jump? Outrider horses don't jump. He's going to be everyone's first choice for the Night Ride now."

I close my eyes. Lean my cheek against Ricochet's bristly mane. This horse was my first choice long before today, and not because he can jump.

"Can't wait for next week's Ride!" The groom kisses Ricochet's nose one last time. "What a pay table that'll be."

My stomach sinks down and down.

Benno is the line judge. Felix is handling the payouts. If they're not behind the Night Ride directly, the jockeys must be well paid for the risk they're taking. Deirdre said she'd handle everything, but Benno and Felix and the others won't want anyone interfering.

They'll find a way to silence her. Maybe for good.

The outrider stable is lit by a dim glow of moonlight from the stall gates, and whoever got here before me put the safety lamps on their lowest setting. I'm crosstying Ricochet when three horseboys slip along the aisle and into the tack room. When I peek around the door, they're already hard at work, wiping down bridles and shaking out saddle pads.

So that's how everything is clean in the morning.

Ricochet's warm breath is damp in my ear, then he's dragging his tongue down my cheek and I giggle and duck away.

Then I step back and just look at him. His soft, velvety ears. His huge dark eyes.

"We won," I say aloud, to him and the dim, empty aisle. "We won!"

This must be how Deirdre feels when she flies over the finish line on a horse like Perihelion or Hesperides. What all the jockeys feel.

What I could feel too if I rode racehorses for the king.

When I reach across Ricochet's haunch with a soft bristle brush, my pocket clanks, and out of habit I hold my other hand against it to quiet the coins.

It's strange to have a dinar when you're used to coppers. Dinars are as big as a plum, and the outline of the king in profile is a firm ridge. Coppers are the size of your thumbnail, and the smudgy lines of the castle are rubbed nearly gone by thousands of fingers.

It's strange to have a dinar, but almost unthinkable to have *five*.

As Ivar comes in with Banner, he pats Ricochet's haunch and murmurs something that sounds like *next time*, and my stomach lurches.

In one week, there'll be another Ride. It'll happen with me or without me, and Deirdre can't help.

Next time, I'll turn up at the outrider stable just as it's getting dark. I won't give any of them a chance to beat me here and take Ricochet. The only way to keep him safe is to ride him myself.

Next time, and every time after that, because it won't do to keep him safe for just a few weeks, or even months. As long as he's an outrider horse at the race-track, Ricochet won't be completely out of danger. That won't happen until he's wearing the red bridle that shows he's mine.

The only way to get him that red bridle is to do the Night Ride.

11

THE NEXT DAY is a race day, and I forget until I turn up at breakfast and there's no food that needs a plate. Just big buttery slabs of toast and fat sandwiches stuffed with egg and bacon and thick mushrooms the size of your palm that you're meant to grab and eat on the way to wherever you're supposed to be.

At the outrider stable, the stablehands split into pairs and take one horse each from a list hastily chalked on a board near the feed cupboard. Lucan and I are partners, and as we catch and crosstie Hollyhock, I keep waiting for him to mention the Night Ride, but all he does is stuff pastry in his mouth as he works the pump.

I don't know how to bring it up, so I just get the horse soap.

"The most important thing is to not be nervous," Lucan says as he dumps a bucket of water over Hollyhock's back. "There'll be a lot of people there to watch the races and it can feel strange, but just remember they're not there for you. You'll be fine if you pay attention to your horse and try not to notice the crowd."

I frown at him, bewildered, until I remember that the top six finishers in the Night Ride get to accompany the king's racehorses on outriders during every race.

"Once Hollyhock is clean, I can finish the braiding," Lucan goes on. "You should probably get changed."

I look down at myself. He must know that I have nothing decent to change into.

"They'll have delivered your gear by now," he adds. "I know you wish you could ride Ricochet today, but a certain trainer will have kittens if that horse is anywhere near Perihelion."

I hesitate, then ask, "Who are *they*?"

"I don't ask questions. Not when all this means my mother will never have to take another hiring fair contract."

Lucan uses words like *all this* to talk about the Night Ride, but the rest of the kids don't seem to care who overhears. If the pay table relies on penny wagers, it's probably better if everyone at the track knows, and no one wants to be the one who ruins it for everyone else.

No one wants to be discovered participating in something that cuts the king out of his twenty shares.

So I pick up a wooden scraper and run it gently but firmly down Hollyhock's rump, pressing extra water out of his coat. Lucan does the same on the gelding's other side, and after a long moment he murmurs, "She worked so hard to raise me by herself. She should get to rest."

You won't be the only one who sends coppers home.

"Hey, you're not riding today with the racehorses, right?" I ask. When Lucan flinches, I wish I could have it back so I could say it nicer, but I go on, "Sorry. What I mean is, would you be willing to do me a favor? I want to send my winnings from last night to my family. Would you deliver it? I'll pay you."

"Don't you want to bring it in person? My mother loves when I can visit for an hour or two." Lucan must see something in my face because he says, "Or maybe you don't have that kind of family."

"No. I do. I just . . . don't think it's good for me to go home right now."

"Even if you bring coppers?"

I cough a laugh. "Dinars, you mean. All of them. That's the only thing that might convince my parents to let me stay at the track."

Lucan's eyes get big. "I thought you were saving for your horse."

"I'm supposed to send home a hundred and fifty coppers a month. If I send all five dinars, I won't have to worry about it for . . ." I squint, trying to figure, then give up. "A while."

"Three months," he replies with a kind smile. "One-fifty, three hundred, four-fifty. With fifty extra coppers left over."

He says it so easily, without a hint of meanness or mocking, that I miss Greta down to my toenails. The Greta who shoveled manure with me and helped work out the value of hooves and shins and fetlocks for a horse she had little interest in.

"My father was pretty mad the last time I was home." I say it lightly, with a carefree shrug. "It's going to be better if he has a chance to calm down. If there's enough money in his pocket, my job will start to make sense to him."

Lucan gently rubs a towel down each of Hollyhock's legs. "I'll deliver your purse, and don't worry about paying me. I'm just happy that you changed your mind about riding with us. I try to like everyone, but some of these guys? I wouldn't want to share a jockey house with them."

I start to remind him about *guys*, but he laughs and adds, "Astrid's okay. But she wouldn't be in the jockey house anyway."

"She wouldn't?"

"Of course not. She's a girl. Deirdre's not allowed anywhere near the jockey house." Lucan frowns. "Didn't you know?"

That little room in the stable that smells like compost. The apple crates and rough-cut window—that's Deirdre's *bedroom*?

"But Astrid and I live in the bunkhouse," I say, slow and puzzled.

"Yeah, well." Lucan scrubs the back of his neck, not looking at me. "I guess it's different when you're older."

I wouldn't mind sleeping in a stable. It would be comforting to drift off every night hearing horses whuffle and whicker and shift in the straw.

I would mind *having* to sleep there while boys got curtains and carpets and real beds.

Once Hollyhock is drying in the sun, I head to the bunkhouse, and sure enough, there's a new set of riding clothes neatly folded on the end of my bed. The shirt is made of linen so fine it's like wearing air, and the buttons are jade. I don't even know what material the breeches are made from. Something soft and stretchy, lined with silk. Something I didn't know existed, straight from a shop on a toll road.

At the end of the bed is a pair of new boots. Soft leather, gracefully tooled with a thick swirly pattern that I belatedly realize is a line of teeny galloping horses, each tinier than half a pinky nail. I change into clean stockings before I try them on, and when I do, I find something cold and solid in each toe.

Toll road tokens. Two rolls of them, wrapped in heavy brown paper.

The riding clothes fit perfectly. The boots make a satisfying *clack* on the wooden floor. Nothing itches. Nothing bags where it should lie flat or pinches when I reach or bend.

I'm halfway to the outrider stable with my winnings

before I realize that these things were waiting in my room. Behind my locked door.

I try not to shiver.

Hollyhock is clean and beautiful, waiting for me in the horseway already saddled. I thank Lucan again, then remind him where on the common he'll find Greta and the ponies. I jangle the soap flake bag one last time, wistfully, then hand it over and climb aboard Hollyhock.

On the way to the receiving barn, I do the figuring. Lucan said I have three months before my family needs coppers from me again. If the Night Ride happens every week when the moon is bright enough to see by, that's three Rides every month. If I win every time, I could have enough money saved for Ricochet before my family goes through the dinars I just sent.

Ten weeks. Ten wins. Ten purses.

The receiving barn is a long white building between the three-quarters turn and the big main grandstand. Horses are gathering already, all kinds and colors, racehorses and companions and outriders. The king's thoroughbreds are there, as well as dozens from other cities and kingdoms and realms. Beyond, the grandstands are still mostly empty, but a few spectators have arrived early to claim good spots.

When I was in the crowd, watching and cheering, I felt part of everything, but by myself out in the open, it's hard not to feel like a limping pony made to walk for the farrier.

Hollyhock and I have been assigned to the last race, which only makes my belly crawl with more worms. There'll be so much waiting, and the last race is the most prestigious. Perihelion will be in it, along with top-shelf champions belonging to kings and empresses and princes.

Paolo spots me and waves from where he's holding a roly-poly mare barely bigger than a pony. She's the color of dry grass, and she's all forelock and bushy tail. Perihelion's new companion looks like a version of him that grew up in the lanes—smaller, scruffier, and a little more knobby in the knees. The big gold stallion is cross-tied nearby while four trainers argue over which blinkers he should wear.

"You look like you're about to pass out," Paolo says with a grin as he walks over. "This is supposed to be fun."

"It is." I smile back, and it's true, mostly, but as the barn fills up with more strange people, I pull toward the horses. "You must be used to it by now. This is my first time."

Paolo pats the mare on the neck. "I knew before I came to the track that there'd be people everywhere, but that didn't make it any easier to deal with."

Before I came to the track. That payday, Paolo told Deirdre that someone missed her, that she could go home whenever she wanted.

But Deirdre's home is in the lanes, and the lanes are

crowded. Most people have big families, and the little houses usually overflow with aunts and grandparents and cousins and friends who have nowhere else to go.

If Paolo came from the lanes, if he knew Deirdre growing up, he'd be used to people being everywhere. Neighbors, street sweepers, rubbish collectors, children of every age and height and color.

"How is Ricochet?" Paolo asks, and the words aren't out of his mouth before I'm back on the Night Ride, flying through the silvered greenwood. Handing the flags to Benno and collecting the winner's purse.

Benno, who's standing outside the last stall of the receiving barn. Deirdre is with him, and their heads are tipped together like they're deep in a serious conversation.

"I'm too late," I whisper.

Paolo calls after me, but I'm off Hollyhock and leading him at a quick walk up the aisle. My new boots echo and thud alongside my galloping heart. I left everything to Deirdre, and she figured out who's behind the Night Ride. She's going to take care of everything, just like she promised.

Only she doesn't know the danger she's putting herself in. There's no way Benno and the others are going to let her ruin their payday.

". . . better than I thought," Deirdre is saying. "You always worry for nothing."

Benno sees me coming. He murmurs something to

her and steps away, moving past me up the aisle, toward Perihelion. As he passes me, he nods the smallest bit.

Like she just confronted him and he knows everything and now there'll be consequences.

Or maybe like he's being friendly. Saying hey to the girl who shattered the pay table and filled a lot of pockets, including his.

"You didn't tell Benno, did you?" I all but collide with Deirdre and drag her into a corner. "About the . . . the problem? With the outriders? Because you can't. Please. Just trust me."

Deirdre's smile freezes. "Sonnia, we talked about this. You said you'd leave it with me. You said you'd let me take care of everything."

"No!" I press close to Hollyhock for moral support. His breath is warm on my hand. "I mean, you don't have to. I know what's going on. I don't think you can help. I don't *want* you to help."

"You know what's going on." It's not a question, and Deirdre doesn't sound shocked, or upset, or even ready to take my side. Just calm. Oddly calm. "What do you plan to do?"

It stops me. I hadn't planned to do anything beyond convince Deirdre to stay out of the jockeys' way. "Well. Ride Ricochet. If I don't, one of the other kids will."

"You're going to . . . keep riding." She's still calm, but hopeful now, in a cautious, feeling-out sort of way.

"For now." But I'm stuck on *what do you plan to do?*

The way she said it, as if I could choose to do something about the Night Ride and it could work.

"For now," Deirdre echoes, in a voice that sends a chill down my back before I remember that this is *Deirdre*, who once showed me how to sew tiny blankets for my wooden toy horses when I was convinced that they were too cold on their shelf in the loft.

It's quiet all of a sudden. I can hear Hollyhock breathing. I wait for her to go on, to tell me how brave I am, or ask how she can help, even though I just told her I didn't want her to.

When she doesn't, the silence starts to press down and I scramble to fill it. "I mean, doing the . . . the thing is a fast way to get the dinars I need to buy Ricochet. And there are other good things. Being here on race day with the outriders, for one. This is probably when kids get their jockey training, right?"

"Jockey training?" Deirdre frowns. "What are you talking about?"

"The junior racing cadre," I reply, and even now I stumble over *cadre*. "We're supposed to be learning to ride racehorses for the king, right?"

Her frown sours. "I don't know who told you that, but it's utter nonsense. Look around. Do you think any jockey here has time for such a thing? Do you think a single trainer will let kids anywhere near horses like these?"

"But how . . . ?"

"Rider." A trainer appears and taps Deirdre on the shoulder. "Time to weigh in."

She nods to him, then hugs me across the shoulders and says, "Hey, I'm glad you're here, okay? You worked hard for this. You're going to be great."

Once she's gone, I lead Hollyhock back to Perihelion's waiting area. Paolo and I chat about little things to fill the time. The trainers are tense but upbeat, and there's nothing to do but wait.

The racehorses go out one by one, race by race. The outriders follow. Of course today wouldn't be when we'd get jockey training. There's too much going on. Too much at stake.

I've been at the track for weeks now. I've spoken to jockeys precisely twice, and neither time was to talk about my racing seat.

Maybe it's one more thing the Night Ride gains you. One more reason to risk something foolhardy and dangerous. Make a good showing—make the pay table interesting—and perhaps the jockeys will pay more attention to you.

The last race is finally called. The crowd noise echoes all the way to the receiving barn. It's a good thing Hollyhock is doing the walking for both of us because my legs feel like bran mash. Grooms get the racehorses lined up in post parade order, with an outrider between each one.

Then it's time.

When we emerge from the long, dim tunnel onto the track, the cheering is one solid roar. The grandstands rise like walls on every side, crammed with excited spectators, and people crowd the rail.

I do what Lucan said. I stare directly between Hollyhock's ears at the stretch of raked dirt in front of me. I don't look at the crowd. Lucan said no one was here for me, but it doesn't feel that way. I can't shake the feeling that every person at the racetrack is staring at me, from lane kids to the king.

Each step around the track feels like ten thousand, but finally—*finally*—we're back to the receiving barn walkway and I can take a full breath.

Jockeys have to do this all the time, and people really *are* looking at them.

Every moment in the saddle is a good moment, but right now I'm happier to be in the receiving barn with Hollyhock, loosening his girth and pumping him some water and telling him what a good boy he is.

Being on the track in front of all those people was a lot less fun than I thought it would be.

Ricochet and I win the next Night Ride. This time, there's no dash to the finish line. We're out front easily, and Ricochet sails over the pasture fence again like a waterfall of shiny coat and flowing tail.

Benno grins as he hands me the winner's purse. Part of me wants to slap that smirk off his face, but mostly

I'm grateful it's there. It means Deirdre has kept well away from the Night Ride. If the first girl jockey for the king of Mael Dunn leaves in disgrace—or worse, disappears completely—there might never be another one.

When race day comes around, I'm paired with Julian to bathe and braid, and when we're almost done, I tell him he should ride in the post parade instead of me.

"You don't want to?" he breathes.

"I got to last time," I say with a shrug, but the crawly feeling of being in a fishbowl climbs up my neck and I shudder. "You don't get a chance very often. Go ahead."

Julian practically skips up the horseway to change. I spend the afternoon with Ricochet in the outrider pasture, working on a new trick. Soon he'll know how to lift a foot on command. The roar of the crowd almost shakes the ground, but I can enjoy it here. I love that people came all this way to watch beautiful horses run.

But when I put down my bowl at supper, the whole table goes quiet. I reach for the milk pitcher and ask, "What? What's wrong?"

"You weren't at the track today," Marcel says. "The jockeys weren't happy."

Julian at the end of the table hunches over his stew.

"Oh. Well. I'm sorry about that, but what does it matter if they're happy? We're doing what they want, aren't we? Every week when the moon is up?"

"There are rules," Astrid replies, "and we have to

follow them. You earn a spot on post parade, you take it. You want a spot, you earn it."

Julian puts down his spoon as if it weighs a thousand pounds, and a dart of anger shoots through me.

"Where's the harm in what I did?" I sweep a glance around the table. "Maybe Julian would win a spot on his own if the jockeys actually taught us things about racing like you said they would."

Marcel frowns. "I never said the jockeys taught us things."

"You did! You said—"

"I said we were training to be jockeys," he cuts in. "You do enough Night Rides, you'll learn *instinct*. Benno says you can't teach that any other way."

I'm floundering. "Well. Maybe. But what about everything else a jockey has to know?" Greta's questions come back in a rush. "How to sit a racing saddle? How to change leads on turns?"

"Benno says any halfway decent rider can just pick up that sort of thing." Lucan smiles at me from across the table. "That means you'll be fine."

My mouth is flopping open. This makes no sense. Deirdre must have learned to ride racehorses because of the junior racing cadre. She surely wasn't raised by bandits, and lane kids eat more horses than they ride.

But if she came up through the cadre, she would have known about the Night Ride. She would never have endangered her position as a jockey by keeping such a thing to herself, and the track stablemaster listens to her.

"Why should we have to *just pick up* any of it?" I ask. "The jockeys are the ones who need us, right? Without us, there's no Night Ride. We could just not do the Ride until they agree to train us."

Lucan's jaw trembles. "Don't even joke about that."

"There'll be a cadre with us or without us," Astrid says. "There'll be a Night Ride, too. What good would it do?"

"If we all refused to ride—"

"Sonnia. We can't. No one at this table." Her voice sharpens. "We go the way the wind blows. All of us."

All of us. The junior racing cadre. Lane kids, every one, flying through the darkest part of night past branches that slice and rocks that trip and rough, uneven ground that could very well snap a fetlock or break a neck.

"Do you understand?" Astrid asks quietly.

I wish I didn't. But I do. I keep my eyes on my supper so I don't glance at Gowan, who's quietly starting his third helping of stew.

At breakfast the next morning, I greet everyone as I put down my oatmeal and fruit. Astrid gives me a brief nod, but lowers her voice and turns toward Marcel so I can't see her face. Lucan is across the table from me, but as I sit, he picks up his bowl and moves to the other end of the bench.

It stings more than it should.

When it's time for lunch, I meet Paolo coming from the racehorse barn and ask if I can sit with him at the horseboy table. I'm dreading telling him why, but he doesn't ask. He doesn't seem to mind that I don't want to talk much at all, simply sliding down on the bench so the friendly chatter surrounds me without needing anything from me.

Ricochet and I place in the next Night Ride, coming in second by half a length to Bertram. The bag Benno hands me this time sags on its drawstrings, but not in a good way. Fifty coppers are half a month's stablehand pay, but it feels like almost nothing after holding the winner's purse.

Placing doesn't help me. I have to win.

We win the next two, though, and soon I have so many coins that I can't keep them in a soap flake bag anymore. Instead I go through stable cupboards till I find an old leather message satchel, the kind fleet riders carry. The money covers the bottom when I pour it in. Dinars make a deep, resonant clank when they hit one another. Nothing like the musical *plinkyclink* of coppers.

I count my winnings every night before I go to sleep. I line them up in rows, dinars first and then coppers. This is figuring I absolutely cannot mess up.

One evening I take my pony ride coppers out of their ratty bag and include them in the count, but they make the rows uneven. The two leftover coins at one end look pitiful, like something a toddler would hold in her grimy fist in line at the doughnut cart.

I sweep the pony ride coppers back into their silly horseshoe bag and shove them deep into my barn jacket's inner pocket, where they stay.

The moon comes up, and Ricochet and I are ready. We take an early lead, but I follow a trail I'm sure is a shortcut and it's long, moonlit moments before I realize we bypassed the craggy rock where the flags are. We have to retrace, and by the end I'm pushing Ricochet so hard that his breath comes uneven when we cross the chalk line. We finish fifth.

"I'm so sorry, friend," I whisper as we walk extra cooling laps around the outrider pasture. "Only a few more wins. I promise."

The best part of any day is still the trail ride, and I drop by the racehorse barn to beg Paolo to come so at least someone will talk to me.

"Give me a moment and I'll meet you there," Paolo says, and nods to the privy behind the barn.

I'm walking up the aisle of the outrider stable when I hear voices in the pasture.

". . . about her," Marcel is saying. "It's pretty obvious she doesn't want to be a jockey."

"I'm not worried," Astrid replies. "She's not going to do anything to mess up the Ride. How can she? Once she buys that horse, she's got to keep him somewhere. The track stablemaster's going to make sure that's expensive. There's no way he's going to let her fall off the pay table."

The track stablemaster . . . knows about the Night Ride?

"She sends coppers home," Lucan offers. "She told me our regular pay isn't enough. The Ride is what lets her keep working at the track."

"See? She'll come around."

The figuring is catching up to me. Astrid's right. Even if Ricochet is my own horse, I'll have to pay to keep him somewhere. That's on top of what I need to give to my family.

But none of that is sending a slow churn of acid through my belly and up my throat. It's one thing to be mad at someone. Another thing entirely to talk about them behind their back.

I never told Lucan it was a secret that I'm sending coppers home, but him saying it outright makes it feel that way. As if he blabbed something I'd rather the others not know. That he cares more about the cadre than he does about being a good friend.

"Hey, are we riding or what?" Paolo appears in the doorway of the stable, grinning like a sunny day, and the voices out back go quiet for a long moment before they call hello.

Paolo gives me a puzzled look, but I put my head down and hurry into the outrider pasture.

The stablehands don't mind Paolo joining us. The

more outriders on the trail, the better. Ricochet trots over when I whistle, and soon we're moving into the greenwood.

I hang back and ride last, well away from the others. Paolo joins me, chatting amiably about how delighted the trainers are that Perihelion won his last race and how the king sent a box of chocolates the size of a water trough for his keepers to share.

I nod when I'm supposed to and mumble *uh-huh* every now and then, but the only thing my mind has room for is how the track stablemaster knows about the Night Ride.

If he knows, it means he's not scrambling to tell the king to keep from being branded and exiled like Deirdre said.

If he's not afraid the king will find out and punish him, it means he doesn't care who else knows. The racetrack operates separately from the royal stables, and grooms and horseboys and trainers can lay wagers on the Night Ride and feel like they're as good as the nobility who can afford to place gentlemanly wagers at the track betting window.

It can mean only one thing. The track stablemaster is behind the Night Ride. He's the one putting the horses at risk so he can fill his pockets without lifting a finger. He's putting *us* at risk, too.

Right now I have forty-two dinars. Two more wins and Ricochet will have that red bridle. The track stablemaster won't have to make his keep expensive just to keep me on the pay table, because if the Night Ride is what it takes to make Ricochet my own and keep him safe, I'll do it.

Then maybe the junior racing cadre will finally accept me as someone who belongs here.

12

"SONNIA." PAOLO TAPS on my bunkhouse door again. "It's almost time. I know you don't love post parade, but Deirdre's pretty sure you're dragging your feet on purpose."

"I'm braiding my hair." I'm not, though. I'm sitting on my bed in my fancy riding clothes, trying to swallow down the swarmy feeling that comes over me every race day. "My helmet doesn't fit right otherwise."

The door isn't closed all the way, and Paolo pushes it open and steps inside.

Lucan would sigh impatiently from the doorway without looking at me. Astrid would glare. But Paolo makes a show of glancing around my little room. "I can understand how you don't want to leave all this luxury! Too bad I'm not allowed to be a stablehand. I could get used to a space that's big enough to turn around in and doesn't smell like horse wind."

I smile even though I don't feel like it because he's trying to cheer me up. I *don't* love post parade, and I love it less every time I have to do it. If I didn't need to win races for the purses, I'd finish last every time just to spite the lot of them.

"I mean, look at all this stuff. A window. With shutters!" Paolo waves his hand toward it like he's never seen one before, then kneels and makes a big show of noticing my apple crate. "And here's a versatile piece of furniture. It can hold all your many possessions. Your barn clothes that belong on the scrap heap. A dress I've never seen you wear. And a leather—wait, I've been looking for that."

I look up at the same moment Paolo hefts my message bag. The flabby drawstrings have never worked well, and the top gapes open to reveal all my coppers and dinars practically bursting into his hands.

Paolo's mouth falls open, and at length he murmurs, "Sure wasn't this way when I last had it."

"Give me that." I grapple the bag out of his hands, trying to cinch the strings closed. "I'm sorry. I didn't know this was yours. I found it in a stable. I'll give it back once I get a different one."

"Keep it. I'll get another. How . . ." Paolo waves a hand like he'll catch the words he wants. "Where did you get all that money?"

I'm sitting on the bed again, holding the bulging bag tight against my stomach. It's not that I think he'll take it. It's that I worked so hard for every dinar. Ricochet, too. Each one is a twisted hoof we avoided. A sharp branch to the eye neither of us got.

"Because the only people I know who have that many dinars at once are bandits," Paolo goes on, in a voice that's sharp enough to bring my head up.

"I'm not a *bandit*," I snap, and the word tastes bad in my mouth.

Paolo folds his arms. He leans against the wall like we have all afternoon and he's willing to wait.

"Come now, you know very well why," I mutter. "Everyone knows. They're perfectly fine with lane kids and outrider horses risking their lives so they can jingle those coppers."

"Sonnia." Calm. Steady. His horse voice. "I honestly have no idea what you're talking about."

I'm not in the mood for teasing, but when you have both an older brother and a younger sister, you know teasing when you hear it, and this is definitely not teasing.

So I tell him what happens every week when the moon is up. By the time I get to the pay table, Paolo's mouth is hanging open once again.

"Wait. Wait." He rocks away from the wall like it just stung him. "Do you mean every one of Deirdre's stablehands rides in this race?"

I open my mouth to correct him, that we're stablehands for the racetrack and not Deirdre's personal hiring fair help.

But when it's time for monthly wages, Deirdre is the one with the cash box.

Instead I nod. "But how do you not know? Perihelion's grooms are always at the pay table. Hesperides' as well. Their exercise riders. Horseboys. I thought *everyone* knew."

Paolo is pacing. One hand pressed to his mouth like he just got punched.

"I know it sounds bad," I say into the silence, "and yeah, it *is* bad, but you should know that—"

"I want to ride." He stops by the door, all good cheer gone. He looks like he's about to face a company of bandits by himself. "What do I need to do?"

"Ah." I was ready to convince him to keep his mouth shut, and I scramble for words. "Why? I have no idea how to get you on the pay table, so even if you win, you probably won't get the purse. You might not even get fair finish coppers."

"I don't want to be on the pay table. In fact, don't tell anyone. Just tell me when and where."

The message bag in my lap is heavy. I pull the strings together, forcing them into a bow that still wants to slide open.

Who am I going to tell? Lucan, who's upset because I suggested he deserves something big and impossible? Astrid, who has made a place in the cadre for herself alone? Marcel, who thinks I'm going to sabotage the one thing that'll let me keep Ricochet? The jockeys, who put horses in danger every week for their own gain?

I set my message bag back in the apple crate and arrange my old school dress on top of it. Then I put on my helmet and look Paolo in the eye. "Tomorrow when the moon is up. Come to the outrider stable after supper and wait for me."

The moon rises slow and big. There's no sign of Paolo anywhere in the outrider stable, or beside it, or behind it. He must have changed his mind.

It's not like I'm going to hold that against him, though.

Ricochet comes at the whistle. One by one, the stablehands catch horses, ready them, and disappear toward the field. None of them look my way.

The moment the last kid is gone, a shadow emerges from the three-sided shelter at the far end of the pasture. Banner comes toward me at a confident canter, Paolo on his back. I'm not sure whether to be relieved or dismayed.

I lead Ricochet through the pasture gate, hold it for Paolo, then close it behind me before mounting up.

"Are you sure about this?" I ask as we ride toward the field.

Paolo nods. He looks fierce, like he's moments from a fistfight, but gutsick, too. I tug the white kerchief out of my barn jacket as we take a position at the end of the shadowy line of stablehands. Julian is on my left, atop Hollyhock. His face is almost as pale as the gelding's coat.

I don't give the kids a chance to notice there's an extra rider. I drop the white cloth and we watch it flutter down.

The kerchief has barely touched the grass when Paolo sends Banner off the line from standstill to gallop in a blink.

It's a long, cluttery, bewildered moment before I realize it's a fair start. The kerchief was down, no question, and Paolo is at least two lengths in front of everyone and gaining by the second.

As if he's done the Night Ride a thousand times.

Cursing, I shift my weight up and forward, which Ricochet knows is a signal to take off fast, like a racehorse off the chalk. We hurtle toward the entrance to the greenwood, but Banner's rump disappears through it well ahead of us.

This can't be happening. I need to win.

The trail is familiar by now, even at night. Especially at night. I know where to trot and where to gallop, and so does Ricochet. We're on a straightaway that I know is well trodden and safe, and I urge him faster and faster.

"We'll catch them at the tight turn," I whisper to Ricochet. "Don't worry. Banner can never stand still."

But when we arrive, there's a gap in the flags where one's been taken from the middle, and Paolo and Banner are already a clack of hooves moving away on the next straight stretch.

None of this makes sense. Paolo's been on the trail a handful of times, but he's riding as if he's led the pay table for years.

Well. I like Paolo and I love Banner, but they are not going to win the Night Ride. Paolo said he didn't even care about the purse.

I do, and I'm not giving it up easily.

Ricochet and I climb the rocky hill and reach the meadow. Paolo and Banner must still be ahead of us because they're nowhere in sight. Julian is two lengths behind me, and we're neck and neck as we move cautiously through the meadow toward the flag bush.

Julian must really want to go on post parade. He's surely not riding timid tonight, though Hollyhock is definitely helping. That horse has heart to spare.

Ricochet and I reach the bush and I grab a flag, but I pull too hard and the bow turns into a knot. While I'm picking it apart, cursing, Julian wheels Hollyhock and they head for the trail.

I curse louder and rip the whole branch off, shoving the thorny thing into my barn jacket where it bites into my side.

We emerge at the last checkpoint to see Hollyhock and Julian disappearing along the straightaway at a canter. I tell Ricochet to stand and untie a flag, carefully this time. When I shove the strip of cloth in my barn jacket, the thorns from the branch carve into my hand.

No time for that. I urge Ricochet forward.

Ricochet and I can catch them on this stretch. I know we can. We'll pass them and Paolo, too, and that purse will be mine.

I shift my weight and Ricochet's strides get longer and it's like his hooves hardly touch the ground and we are flying.

But we're not flying fast enough, and Hollyhock and Julian are two lengths ahead of us. As we come up the last part of the trail, the back pasture appears in bigger and bigger spans, but there's no sign of Paolo walking Banner cool.

Which means Julian is leading the Night Ride, and all it'll take to win is getting in front of him.

We're approaching the track gate, which I now know is open because of the Ride and not because of some careless groom or horseboy.

Julian doesn't head for it, though. Instead he rides straight for the pasture fence.

Like he means to jump.

Hollyhock takes off, the moonlight glancing off his haunches, and for a moment there's nothing more gorgeous, even if it means we'll only place instead of win.

Then his front hooves catch the top rail with a hard *clatterthud*. He pitches over the fence straight into the ground like a bag of wet sand and lies there flailing and screaming.

Julian struggles clear and scrabbles backward as Hollyhock tries to get his legs under him, grinding out a neighscream that sends a cold chill down my back.

I steer Ricochet toward the gate and wrestle him into a canter. There's no way I'm going to let him jump now. I can barely keep my supper down.

The finish line is ahead and Benno's waiting at the chalk. We have a clear path and it's five dinars closer, but already I'm reining in Ricochet as sharp as he can manage even as Ivar and Gowan thunder toward the gate almost as one.

I slow Ricochet as we approach Hollyhock, then I slide down and edge near. The gray gelding is on his feet again, his saddle loose and hanging awkwardly over his flank, but he's favoring his front foreleg.

"Hollyhock missed the jump." Julian appears at my side, one hand pressed to his mouth. "Ricochet never misses a jump."

"Hollyhock's not Ricochet," I reply in my horse voice, easy and mellow, but every part of me is ready to explode like a pot with a too-tight lid.

Another set of hooves drum behind us, only these slow and stop and then Paolo is at my elbow, holding Banner's reins. He keeps whispering *I don't believe this*, like I hadn't told him exactly what to expect.

I'm close enough to Hollyhock to lay a hand on his neck. He startles and grunts, but he lets me take the reins. He lets me run unsteady hands down his shoulder and onto his back, loosening the tie strap and letting the whole saddle tumble to the ground.

"This is my fault," Julian whispers.

"Not helpful now." Horse voice. Calmly. "What would be helpful is you cooling down Ricochet so I can look Hollyhock over."

"Take Banner, too," Paolo says, and Julian nods numbly and takes both sets of reins. He joins the others cooling their horses along the inside of the pasture fence.

Hollyhock is holding one hoof off the ground. His nose is pointed that way too, and his ears are slack and listless. He's calmer now, grunting that horrible noise faint and tired instead of neighing it.

Paolo keeps muttering *unbelievable*, both hands pushed through his moon-edged hair, before breaking away and storming toward Benno.

I let Hollyhock smell my hand, murmuring calming things, then run whisper-gentle hands down his injured leg. If a bone is sticking out, nothing can be done for him.

"Didn't you see them fall?" Paolo stands in front of Benno like a prizefighter. "That horse is hurt and someone needs to help him!"

Benno sighs. "He'll be fine or he won't. They're just outrider horses. There's more where they came from. Just take your money and go to bed, all right?"

They're just outrider horses.

Perihelion's head trainer heaves himself over the fence and approaches Paolo, dropping a hand on his shoulder like an uncle would, or a big brother. There's a murmur of conversation, far away like hooves in a distant pasture.

There's more where they came from.

There'll be a Night Ride with or without Hollyhock, too.

Julian edges near, Banner and Ricochet trailing behind. I can barely look at this boy. He hands me Ricochet's reins, then stands awkwardly a length away like I'm bigger than I am.

"Is it bad?" Julian whispers.

I shrug, short and stabby. "Nothing's obviously broken. No deep cuts. But what do I know, right?"

"I shouldn't have tried to jump him," Julian murmurs. "I just . . . all those guys cheer when Ricochet jumps. *Trainers* cheer. Real trainers of real racehorses. Guys who'll be judging the jockey tryouts. No one but you gets to ride Ricochet. And I'm a terrible person."

I try to glare at him, but I can't. Julian and me, Astrid, Lucan, every kid in the cadre—all of us have white on our foreheads and feet. We've always been meant to be ground up for someone else's benefit.

"*You're* not the terrible person," Paolo growls as he appears on the other side of Hollyhock's sweaty neck. "Foolish, maybe, but you've got an excuse. Deirdre doesn't."

I try to catch Paolo's eye. The last thing I need is for Julian to run to Deirdre and drag her back into the middle of this.

But Paolo is murmuring to a groom standing a pace behind him, a wiry graybeard who's hunched like a beetle, wringing and folding his hands. The old man reaches for Hollyhock's reins and makes soft cooing sounds as he coaxes the gelding away, step after shambling step.

Soon there'll be a nice comfortable bed of straw for that poor horse, and leg wraps, salt soaks, treats. The doctors will rush over and figure out how to help him.

"Sonnia?" Julian shuffles uncomfortably. "Is it true? Do you really not want to be a jockey?"

"No." It comes out swift and honest. "I don't care about racing. I don't care about winning. I just want to ride."

Julian is quiet for a moment. "Then can I tell you a secret? I don't really want to be a jockey, either."

I look up, startled, and he goes on, "But I love the junior racing cadre. I'm never lonely here. Never scared. I know what tomorrow's going to look like, and the day after that, and I get paid in the bargain. Would a terrible person help you get all that?"

"Deirdre," I whisper, and he nods.

"None of this is her fault," Julian goes on. "Deirdre's the best one of them."

The crowd around the pay table is gone, along with

the table itself and Benno and the strongbox and a single hint that anyone was here only an hour ago. The other kids in the cadre have led their horses back to the outrider stable, and Julian hurries down the horseway after them. The pasture is empty and the moon fills the sky, and I shiver.

I turn to ask Paolo how he seemed to know exactly what to do on the Night Ride, but he's gone.

He's gone before I can ask why he'd been so determined to do it at all.

He's gone before I can find out what he meant about Deirdre.

13

I BARELY SLEEP, and when the sky lightens enough to see, I get dressed and hurry toward the racehorse barn. I have to get to Paolo before he confronts Deirdre.

But his stuffy closet-sized room is empty. It's not just that Paolo isn't here. His room has nothing in it—no clothing or boots or blankets on the bed.

It's like he packed everything and left.

Deirdre isn't in her room either, but there's a pile of slept-in bedclothes on the floor and a hairbrush on the crate. A groom tells me she went to the track for morning exercise runs.

I'm not too late. She's still a jockey.

There's a new horse in Hollyhock's stall. A sassy bay mare with a forelock that needs trimming who takes delight in trying to eat buttons off your jacket like they're treats, but who definitely *isn't* Hollyhock.

The other kids get to work with shovels and buckets like nothing is out of the ordinary.

They're just outrider horses. There's more where they came from.

After breakfast, I head to the animal hospital. Paolo might have gone there to check on Hollyhock. It's in a part of the track complex I've never been to, on the eastern side beyond the first turn where there are beautiful barns and living quarters for the foreign racehorses and their keepers who come from other kingdoms to compete for purses and prizes.

The animal hospital is a sprawling whitewashed building that smells like bleachy water and antiseptic rub. Inside, there are eight stalls, four on each side of a wide concrete aisle. Three are empty, and racehorses stand or lie in the others. I know they're racehorses because there's no mistaking one for an outrider, even when they're sick or hurt.

None are gray, and none are geldings. There's no sign of Hollyhock.

This doesn't make sense. If he's not in his stall in the outrider stable, there's nowhere else they might have taken him.

A doctor with a clipboard appears in the aisle. I've never seen anyone with cleaner hands or a tidier beard. He peers over a stall door, then his pencil goes flying over a sheet of thick paper. I can't stop staring. He must have been *years* at school to write that fast, when it takes me an age to print my name.

"What are you doing here, kid?"

All at once he's next to me, *above* me, towering like a cranky, twenty-hand stallion with the same angry, flaring nostrils.

"Sorry. Sir. I just came to see a horse who got hurt." I curtsy with the ends of my tunic.

The flaring stops and the doctor's face relaxes, but he still looks wary. "It's not about some outrider horse, is it? Honestly, the last kid who was here didn't seem to understand that this is the royal animal hospital and we treat racehorses here. Racehorses only."

"The last kid?" I'm suddenly hopeful. "A boy with brown skin? Blue shirt? Did you see where he went?"

The doctor coughs a laugh. "Took off from here like he was on fire when he found out that limping gray gelding he was yelling about was long gone to the butchery pens."

"Wait." Something cold is crawling down my spine. "If only racehorses get treatment here, where do outrider horses go when they get hurt?"

"I just told you."

"No," I whisper, because if Hollyhock could walk away last night, he likely just needs rest and splints and lots of hot bran mash.

"If you find that kid, tell him to save his breath," the doctor goes on. "The track stablemaster isn't going to punish Deirdre for what happened to that outrider horse. Deirdre could be burying bodies in the pasture and the track stablemaster would ask if she needs a better shovel."

I stumble out of the hospital. Past racehorses resting comfortably with grain in their feedboxes and smelling of muscle rub.

Past three open stalls.

I tell the other stablehands that I have a stomachache. It's not entirely a lie, and I do go to the bunkhouse, but it's not to rest. Instead I put on my fancy riding clothes, collect a handful of toll road tokens, and head for the city gates.

Cobbles disappear beneath my feet. Sheer marble buildings catch the sun and wink. My stomach turns just at the thought of the butchery pens, much less a horse I know and love trapped there, but if I don't find Paolo, he's going to say something he shouldn't to someone he shouldn't, and all of us are done for.

Soon I reach the northern gate of the city, and outside, the market spreads in tents and stalls and carts across big fields all the way to the greenwood. The animal pens are at the edge, inside a fence made of ropes strung taut, and I hurry past the sheep and goats and chickens, straight to the horses.

The draft horses are first, giants with glorious feathery hair over their hooves who pull plows and harrows through fields of wheat or barley. Then saddle horses, proud and lively, and then cart horses packed from shoulder to haunch with muscle. Last are the pony pens, where a very small me chose Buttermilk because I'd never seen any animal the color of a perfect sunrise.

The butchery pens are tucked away so you have to mean to go there. There's no shade and only one water trough, and the horses are bony and pitiful. Hollyhock stands near the front, holding his hoof off the ground. His coat is sweaty and filthy from the Ride. I lean over the fence to pet him, and he gives a weary nicker.

"Two dinars. Firm price." A dealer oozes over. He's got a thin greasy moustache and a smile that only a fool would trust.

I pull my hand away from Hollyhock's neck, but it's too late. The dealer knows I'm not here for meat.

I have money, but not with me. Even if I could get it, there's nowhere to keep this poor horse if he's not welcome at the outrider stable.

"Fifty coppers," says a voice from behind me. "Both of us know he's not the first and he won't be the last."

I whirl, and there's Paolo. He's wearing a leather tunic like rangers have, or fleet riders, or bandits, and his boots are caked in mud.

I'm about to say how glad I am to see him, to pour out everything that needs saying, but something in his face warns me away from it.

The dealer glances between us slow and suspicious. He's worried he's being tricked. Paolo and I don't look related, though, and my friend is acting like I don't exist.

Which I belatedly realize is the point.

At length the dealer says, "One dinar. Both of us know this horse ended up here for a reason."

"Done." Paolo drops a big gold coin into the dealer's leathery palm, and the old man steps into the pen to fetch Hollyhock.

He's not the first. When I started at the outrider stable, there was a little roan mare with a cracked hoof. Jubilee. Lucan said he'd take care of it, and then she was gone, and she surely didn't go to the animal hospital.

He won't be the last. I stare hard at my feet. It could have been Ricochet.

It could still be Ricochet.

Paolo takes the lead rope from the dealer and *click-clicks* to Hollyhock. Together they begin shambling step by limping step toward the exit.

I trot to catch up. "Where are you taking him?"

"Somewhere he'll be safe. Somewhere he'll recover."

"We need to talk. About the Night Ride." I take a deep breath. "About Deirdre."

"It's not supposed to be this way, you know," Paolo growls. "When you ride trails at night, you're supposed to do it as a group. As a *cadre*. For her to use that word, too!"

"When you—*what*? No one should have to do anything like the Night Ride. It's pure foolishness. Pure greed."

"It's not foolish if you do it safely," he replies, low and cold, "and there's no greed without purses or a pay table."

He says it so firmly, like it's something everyone knows, or ought to know. But it's nothing from the lanes. Nothing from Mael Dunn's struggling quarters.

"I—I don't understand," I finally say. "Who else but us does the Night Ride?"

"Riding trails by moonlight is how bandits train," Paolo says, "but they don't race and there's no reward. You start slow, walking, and each night you ride faster. You get to know your horse like a best friend, so you know what they're going to do before they do it, and vice versa."

I trail to a stop. The market carries on around me, past me, animals bleating and people calling and footfalls pattering. There's only one way for Paolo to know all this, and I go still like a spider under a hovering boot.

"Now's the time to yell for a constable if you're going to," he mutters. "Everyone knows how terrible bandits are."

The word still sends a chill down my back, but this is the boy who let a stranger ride Ricochet with him to the racetrack without a second thought, and stood up for Ricochet when Perihelion's trainer threatened the butchery pens. The boy who made a place for me at his table when the stablehands turned their backs.

"Is that where you're taking Hollyhock?" I whisper.

"A bandit camp? And he'll be safe there? Someone will take care of him till he recovers?"

Paolo hitches a shoulder and looks away. Just like I might if a constable stopped me and demanded what I knew about my neighbor's illegal water barrel, or exactly how many children lived in the house down the block.

So I say, "When you grow up in the lanes of Mael Dunn, you know the surest way to make a bad situation worse is calling the constables."

For several moments Hollyhock's hooves seem very loud on the packed dirt between us.

Then Paolo meets my eye steady on and half-smiles. "Spoken like a true bandit. Did you know I thought you were one of us? When we met outside the royal stables? But you didn't motion back." He makes that gesture of his, bringing his hands to his belly button like he's holding reins.

So that's how Paolo knew how to do the Night Ride so well. He's done something like it before. Many times.

"I mean, you seemed to know Deirdre," he adds, "and I thought maybe I wasn't the only one sent to find her after she disappeared from camp."

I can't help but flinch, being mistaken for a bandit, but I tell him, "There's no truth to that rumor. There can't be. Deirdre wasn't raised by bandits. She grew up two streets over from me."

"Depends on what you mean by *raised*." Paolo leads Hollyhock around a chuckhole. "Deirdre lived in my family's camp for three years. My sisters taught her to ride." He must notice my flapping fish-mouth, because he adds, "Bandit life's not what people think."

"Your sisters?" I echo. "Girls get to be bandits?"

Paolo grins. "Girls make the *best* bandits. I'd rather ride with girls than boys any day."

I still don't want to be a bandit, but I can see how a girl from the lanes might. I can see how Deirdre would.

"Honestly?" He squints. "I should have suspected the moment I met Astrid. There's no way the track stablemaster would allow a girl to be a stablehand. But if she also made a pay table interesting? Deirdre would have had no trouble getting Astrid into the junior racing cadre."

"Kids don't just get to be in the cadre," I tell him. "When I was brought in, I had to pass a test. Deirdre had nothing to do with it."

"Are you sure?"

If you do take this job, you can't make me look bad.

We stood in the dusty stable, me clinging at a wispy chance to work with horses, to be near Ricochet. Surely she'd meant the stablehand job.

"Wait." I cut a glance at Paolo. "You can't be saying that Deirdre's a part of the Night Ride. Can you?"

"No," he replies. "I'm saying she's *running* it."

"But that—that's not right. The track stablemaster is behind the Night Ride." I say it firmly, but there's a rasp in my voice.

Paolo gives me the same patient look that Greta does when she's long since figured something out and she's waiting for me to catch up.

"You get a wage to work at the track, right?" he asks. "Ever wonder why it doesn't come from the paymaster?"

Deirdre used to make us pancakes in the shape of animals. She painted our toenails with homemade dye that stained her fingertips bright red for a solid week.

"Ever wonder why no one in the junior racing cadre comes from a riding family, or even a caretaker family? Kids who are supposedly learning to ride racehorses for the king? Ever wonder why every last one comes from the hungriest, darkest corners of the lanes?"

Astrid knew I was saving for Ricochet before I told anyone here. The track stablemaster listens to Deirdre, and they have a common interest in dinars. When Deirdre found out I didn't want her help with the Night Ride, she asked what I planned to do. Somehow my wages after room and board are not enough to let me simply be a stablehand. The only proper jockey training any kid in the cadre will get comes from the Night Ride.

Lane kids have to go where the wind blows.

Paolo and I have reached the place where the tidy road that leads to the market fades into the rough dirt trail that disappears into the greenwood. He turns to me and makes a show of bowing. "I guess this is farewell."

"You're not coming back to the racetrack, are you?" I whisper.

"My parents sent me to find Deirdre, and I did." Paolo studies his feet. "They'll be glad to know she's alive and well, but now that I know what she's doing, I can't stay."

"But you could stop her," I protest. "*We* could stop her. We could save all the outrider horses!"

Paolo smiles. He *clickclicks* to Hollyhock, and together they start down the sun-dappled path. Over his shoulder he says, "I can save *this* horse."

14

WHEN I GET back to the racetrack, it's late afternoon and the day is fading. The stablehands will be on their trail ride, which is just as well. I don't think I can face any of them. I need to see Ricochet.

But he's not in the outrider pasture. Not among the herd. Not in the shelter.

I tear into the stable, knocking over a pitchfork and jostling the rack of currycombs, scattering straw, down the aisle and out the back door—

Ricochet is crosstied under the overhang close behind the stable. Deirdre is running a soft bristle brush over his rump.

I skid to a stop. My heart pounding in big, heavy thumps.

"So." Deirdre doesn't turn. "An eventful Ride last night, wouldn't you say?"

She's not pretending she doesn't know. She's telling me she knows I know.

"It was awful," I whisper, but then I realize she can't hear me, and I risk another few steps closer. "You said you'd take care of everything. You promised."

"Taking care of everything is all I've ever done my whole life. At least now I get something out of it."

Deirdre still hasn't turned, so I move to Ricochet's other side so she has to look at me. She shuffs the brush over his flank like she's seasoning a roast. There's no love in the action. Just efficiency.

I wait, my arms folded tight across my belly, because I want her to deny it. I want her to drop the comb and rush over to hug me like she did when I was small and I would pretend she was our biggest sister who was also a princess and could invite us to have tea with the king.

"You know how much your mother used to pay me to mind you and your brother and sister?" Deirdre meets my eyes over Ricochet's back. "Ten coppers a week. To watch three kids under seven every bleeding day from before dawn till after sundown. Make food. Change diapers. Keep you all busy. Clean up your messes. The bandit camp had a lot of ridiculous rules, but it was a million times better than that crappy job."

That crappy job.

Teaching us how to draw a hopscotch grid in the packed dirt near the rain barrel. Holding Greta up so she could pick an apple off a tree just like the big kids.

"But I took care of that, too," Deirdre growls. "My stablehands make twice that for way less work. They get food and shelter, better and more reliable than the lanes can offer. They get a little time every day to do whatever they want. They get dinars, too, if they can win them."

My stablehands. Deirdre with the cash box on her knees at payday. The same box on the Night Ride's pay table.

"How . . . ?" I choke. Paolo was right. The Night Ride is Deirdre's work. But not the Deirdre I remember.

She shrugs. "More easily than you might think. I told you that the track stablemaster and I share a common interest. Turns out the other jockeys do as well. Everyone likes feeling coins in their pockets."

"No." My voice sharpens. "I meant how could you do this to us? You know how it feels to be where I am. How can you take advantage instead of helping?"

"I have nothing that I didn't suffer to gain," Deirdre snaps.

"Then shouldn't that make you want to help *more*? Because you know how bad it feels to suffer?"

Deirdre cackles. "You're free to leave any time you want. By all means, go back to the lanes and suffer away. Take hiring fair contracts till you crumble over dead. Grow old there with nothing to show for it."

"But what about the horses?" I protest. "Hollyhock got hurt pretty bad. Next time it could be worse!"

"What happened with Hollyhock was ugly, and I'm

sorry for it." Deirdre picks a puff of chestnut hair out of the brush bristles. "But things like that only happen when people choose to behave recklessly."

I'm stuck on too much at once. *People* means more riders than just Julian, *things* means horses being hurt, and *like that* means horses are injured so often that they simply become things.

"You promised to do what you were told and not ask questions," she goes on. "Clearly that didn't happen. So now the question is, what about this boy here?"

Deirdre pats Ricochet on the haunch in what would be a loving gesture if her smile wasn't so cold.

"You almost have enough to buy him, right?"

I nod. "Two more wins."

"What a day that'll be, yes? You'll want to keep him here, I'm sure. You'll want to ride him and be with him. And that can happen. It absolutely can." Deirdre pauses the brush and leans both forearms against Ricochet's back. "Here's the thing, though. The Night Ride is how a lane kid makes that happen. If the Ride goes away, those kinds of things will too. Those will be the *first* things to go away."

I go still. The track stablemaster listens to Deirdre, and no one would miss one outrider horse that somehow disappeared from the pasture.

No one who mattered, anyway.

I shuffle and whisper, "I understand."

"Good." Deirdre tosses me the brush and smiles, and

it's her real smile, the one I remember so well. "I'm going to tell you something I probably shouldn't. You're a natural at the Night Ride. Easily the best in the cadre. You make split-second decisions amazingly well and you don't panic when things go wrong. Not only have you not made me look bad, you've earned me a lot of credit."

Two days ago, I would have drunk that up like honey water. Now I just nod and step to Ricochet's side and start brushing his other flank. I put my whole attention into it until Deirdre's hollow bootsteps fade into the horseway.

Then I put my arms around his neck and breathe out long and shuddery.

"We're stuck," I whisper into his mane. "You'll have your red bridle, but you won't be safe. Not unless I keep doing the Night Ride."

Ricochet is a good listener, but his best advice is a mouthful of hay from the hanging net.

I step back so I can see all of him, from his unlucky white forehead to his unlucky white feet. His big brown eyes.

Beyond him in the pasture are the other outrider horses. Mandalay and his sweet tooth. Gladiola and her sense of fun. Banner and his endless willingness to please. Calpurnia, who loves the company of cats.

It's only a matter of time before one of them follows Hollyhock to the butchery pens, and Paolo won't be there to save them.

Or worse could happen. Then there'd be a single gunshot.

Next time it could be one of us.

In a week, the moon will be up. I'll be expected to join the others. To make the pay table interesting. Like Hollyhock was never here.

Like all of this is okay somehow, as long as you can make excuses. As long as there's money to be made.

As long as I can maintain Ricochet in comfort and safety, even though it means the other outriders are left to take the risk.

As long as I can pretend I'm not the same as these outrider horses. That I won't end up at the hiring fairs once I get hurt bad enough and can't make a pay table interesting.

One thing is certain. The king doesn't know about the Night Ride because no one at the track wants him to find out. No one wants to be branded and exiled, and no one wants to lose out on a few extra coppers in their pockets or the excitement of how they get there.

"What if someone tells the king?" I whisper to Ricochet. "What if *I* tell him?"

Deirdre really wanted me to believe I'd be punished if that happened. That if the king found out, he'd be so angry that no one—not even kids—would escape hot metal and an armed escort outside the city walls.

Deirdre wanted me to believe a lot of things, but horse harm is horse harm.

Unless Master Harold was standing there with me. He's all but Father's big brother, and he's always cared about me and Greta and Torsten like we were his own. He may have spent his one big ask, but maybe just him being next to me will soften the blow.

I'll go tomorrow. First light, before morning chores. Before I lose my nerve.

Only Deirdre isn't a fool. She'll be watching the outrider stable closely now—watching *me*—and no matter what any stablehand tells her, if I'm gone, she'll suspect what I'm doing.

Before I even get to the royal stables, every jockey and groom and horseboy will be ready to deny all knowledge at a formal inquest.

When I confess, Ricochet has to be somewhere safe.

There's no way I can just lead him away from here in broad daylight, though. Someone would notice and stop me. I'm not wearing the king's badge, and Ricochet doesn't have a red bridle or any kind of royal saddlecloth that says I have permission to ride him. It would look like I was stealing him.

There aren't many hanging crimes in Mael Dunn. Just murder, treason—and horse thievery.

Ricochet flicks his tail. He's relaxed and content, one ear swiveled at me, because he trusts me to take care of him and he likes us being together.

It's got to be tonight. Before Deirdre works out what I'm doing.

Before I think too much on how breaking up the Night Ride and saving the outrider horses also means there'll be no more junior racing cadre. Probably no more stablehands, either, if they're paid out of Deirdre's own purse. No more coppers to send home. No more post parades and hope for a future riding racehorses. It'll be back to the lanes and the hiring fairs for all of them.

Before I picture the king's reaction as I tell him everything.

Ricochet and I will head up to the meadow. From there we can travel through the greenwood under cover of darkness till we reach the northern city gate. I'll ask the guards to get Master Harold and I'll turn myself in. Ricochet's old stall is probably waiting. Nice and clean. He can go back to being a fleet horse.

I choke on a sob and press my forehead into Ricochet's shoulder. He'll be safe. Torsten will take good care of him.

I wish I could be as sure about what'll happen to me.

I'm supposedly sick, which gives me an excuse to skip evening chores and supper. I'm on my bed in the bunkhouse impatiently watching the sky darken when there's a knock on my door. It's Astrid, and she's carrying a tray.

"I brought you a mug of broth," she says, "and some fizzy water that might help calm your stomach."

I take the tray and thank her.

She shrugs. "The cookhouse ladies told me I had to."

So Astrid is still upset about what happened with post parade. Or rather, how I suggested perhaps we shouldn't simply do whatever we're told without thinking it through. I almost laugh—soon enough it won't matter—but instead I walk back to my bed to put down the tray.

My steps echo on the wooden floor. Astrid's eyes go to my feet, and I belatedly realize that I'm still wearing my good riding boots and fancy clothes, which are not things people wear when they're sick in bed.

"I needed the privy," I say, and it's too sharp, too defensive.

Astrid shrugs big and showy, complete with eye roll, and disappears out the bunkhouse door.

I drink the broth. It's chicken, hot and delicious. It does help calm my stomach, but not the way the cookhouse ladies intended.

Astrid is mad at me. When Greta is mad at me, she makes a point of ignoring me. Not watching everything I do.

This is going to work. It has to work.

I take off my boots and get under my blankets, though. Just in case.

When my window is finally dark and the bunkhouse has been quiet for some time, I get up and put on my barn jacket over my fancy clothes. It looks mismatched, but a white shirt is too easy to spot in the dark.

Then I kneel next to my apple crate, push aside my old clothes, and pull out my message bag full of clanking, jangling coins. I cinch the drawstrings, but the ancient leather has been worn smooth and the knot slides apart. Growling curses, I strap the bag across my body extra tight. Hopefully that'll keep it quiet as well as safe.

At the very least, Master Harold can see that Father and Mother get this money and they won't have to worry about the rent for a while.

The horseway stands quiet in its wash of silver light, but without the other kids and the jittery excitement of the Night Ride, saddling Ricochet in the dim feels wrong somehow, like I'm a bandit bent on thievery and the moon and stars are here to catch me out.

Once we're in the greenwood, Ricochet wants to gallop the straightaway like he always does, but I make him trot. My leather bag jangles like a charm bracelet, but at least no one's around to notice. Dapples and drips of starlight flash past, and the night air smells clean and vibrant.

Past the stream. Up the hill. It's strange to be out here without anyone to race against. Bandits have the right idea—it's not the worst thing to ride in the dark if you're not trying to win dinars and risking your neck. The night is peaceful, and I never thought I'd come to like it. I never thought I'd like being this far from Edge Lane, where the dark is welcoming instead of scary.

By the time we get to the meadow, everything is still.

No frantic hoofbeats behind us. No thrash of brush. No squeak of leather.

I close my eyes and breathe in the rich, glorious night.

Ricochet clunks the bit between his teeth. He's not sure what to make of us stopping in the meadow. He wants to run, I can tell. He knows the trail and he wants to win.

It's enough to remind me what's at stake.

We circle the meadow, and as we do, I remember my first trail ride when I was here alone because the others wanted to see what kind of rider I was. They'd have reported back to Deirdre, certainly, and she'd have nodded and told Marcel to bring me in.

It had been a test. Just not quite like I thought.

That was the day Hollyhock and I found the beginnings of a path, one he hadn't liked. One that just might be a bandit trail.

Bandit life may be different than I think, but not every bandit is Paolo or his sisters.

Once we head down this path, there's no turning back. Everything I'd hoped to gain here, to build here—gone. And there's still a good chance the king will punish me alongside everyone else.

Ricochet tosses his head. Like he's trying to look me in the eye and remind me that we're doing the right thing.

I knew from the first moment I saw him that we

were meant to be together. He was the lane kid of the royal stables with his unlucky white forehead and feet.

I nudge my knees into his sides, and together we step into the greenwood.

15

THE TREES ARE thick and dense, and we haven't gone far before I realize just how helpful those trails are that we ride every day. A never-ending trample of hooves has removed most of the dangers there—loose stones, stray branches, trailing vines that look like snakes—and even though Ricochet is a fleet horse, I'm not a fleet rider. I'm scared he's going to get hurt, so now he's nervous too. He tosses his head and snorts, and reluctantly I let him walk.

On we go, step on step, through the silver-dappled stillness.

Soon I'm going to be standing before Master Harold. At first he'll be worried, me hustled into his presence—with my wrists bound, perhaps?—and guardsmen frowning like falcons.

If I want him to help me, I'll have to tell him everything. Not just about Deirdre and what she's done. Not just about the jockeys and the track stablemaster and the pay table.

I'll have to tell him I was one of the riders. That I've known about the Night Ride for months and I'm only now coming forward.

I'll have to tell him why.

Master Harold is my father's friend. When I was small, he gave me horsey rides on his shoulders up and down Edge Lane. Sometimes he lets me watch foals being born, and once in a while I get to name the baby.

But Master Harold is the royal stablemaster, and he will not stand before the anointed sovereign of Mael Dunn and defend horse harm.

I'll have a royal audience all right, but I will be entirely on my own.

Ricochet's footfalls go from squishy to hollow, and branches abruptly stop dragging over my face. This must be a bandit trail. Ricochet would be a tempting prize for them. He's a sturdy horse, strong and healthy, and fleet trained.

"They wouldn't be this close to the city," I say to Ricochet. "Too many rangers. Too risky."

Something behind us goes *cracklesnap.*

I go still, and it happens again. The shuffle of footsteps—human or horse, I can't tell, but they're approaching at a steady, determined pace.

Astrid saw me in my riding boots. When Torsten is mad at me, he makes sure I know it.

He makes sure *everyone* knows it.

I curse aloud and urge Ricochet into a trot, then a canter. If I'm caught, there's no reason I can give for being out here.

A branch digs into my hair and jerks my braid loose, and hair whips into my eyes. My leather message bag loosens and bounces, *shinkshink, shinkshink,* and I try to hold it against my ribs with one forearm while steering Ricochet.

Behind us, the footfalls grow louder. Clearer. Whoever it is, they're gaining on us.

The bandit trail ends abruptly, and we're suddenly plunged into the greenwood and its rocky, cluttered ground. Ricochet neighs, startled and frustrated, but instead of slowing, he puts his head down and cuts through the trees.

I'm sliding in the saddle, jolted by both his strange, side-hopping canter-trot, and the heavy motion of the message bag that's coming looser with every step.

I'm grappling for a handhold on the reins to slow him down, stop him, at least guide him out of this minefield of rocks and fallen branches and every other thing that might harm him.

The strap on my message bag snaps. Heavy leather scrapes down my ribs toward the ground. I scrabble to catch the end of the strap, but the fat leather pouch at the other end swings wide and hits a tree.

There's a sound like a thousand chains being dropped

at once, and coins spray in all directions. For a brief, heart-stopping moment I can see each one, lit with thumbnails of silver light from the glitter of stars, before they pass into darkness and disappear softly into the grass and the brush and the undergrowth.

Ricochet is still hurtling down some path of his own making, the empty message bag pattering against his haunch. I can only hold on, but I'm numb.

Every dinar from the winner's purse. Every fair-finish copper. Everything I had to show for the Night Ride—gone.

I haul on the reins, and Ricochet comes to a stumbling, shambling halt. Turning. Panting.

I could scramble down and scratch around on the forest floor. My knees wet. Dirt beneath my nails. Maybe I'd find a coin or two. There's no way I'd find them all.

Especially not before the footsteps find me.

"Go, friend," I whisper into Ricochet's mane, and I nudge him with my calves. He flings himself forward, tossing his head, and I lean low over his neck, shift my weight into racing position, and let the wind blast my tears away.

We ride. Step on step. Walk, trot, walk, canter, until the greenwood is quiet but for us alone. Whoever was following must have given up.

Which means I have to assume Deirdre knows I ran with Ricochet. If it wasn't Astrid chasing me, it was someone else from the cadre that Deirdre sent. I have to get to Master Harold first thing, right when the city gates open, before she can put a stop to what I'm doing.

The horizon is just beginning to think about paling, but the stars still own the sky. My eyelids keep getting heavier. My feet, too. I hope we're not lost. I've been trying to keep a steady path, but I'm a lane kid. I know how to haggle at the market and make broth out of turnip ends. The greenwood and I are new to each other.

It's getting colder, and even though I'm wearing a jacket and boots, I'm starting to shiver.

The northern city gate can't be too much farther.

When Ricochet is cool enough, I let him drink from a stream in small mouthfuls so he doesn't get sick. His sides are glistening with sweat, and it occurs to me that I'm going to hand over an exhausted, bedraggled, famished horse to Master Harold in a few hours, just before I beg him to put in a good word for me with the king.

Step on step. I'm leading Ricochet now, walking next to him. My beautiful boots squish above the ankles in unseen mud. Somehow I kept hold of the empty message bag, and it sags off my shoulder from its knotted-together strap.

I'm stumbling and bleary when a sharp line of dark stone breaks through the round prickliness of the greenwood tops. A turret. The walls of Mael Dunn are just beyond the tree line, and I could cry with relief.

I could cry for a lot of reasons.

When I finally arrive at the northern city gate, it stands well barred and there are no guards at sentry. Too early to give myself up.

I swear aloud and sink to the ground, bringing the reins with me. I've been giving things up one at a time for a while now.

My stablehand job. The junior racing cadre.

The warm, happy memories of those afternoons when Deirdre had us invent games in the backyard that kept us running and chasing and tumbling and laughing.

The money I saved from the Night Ride, every coin of it, all the while convincing myself that what I was doing was okay as long as I had a good reason.

Now Ricochet. Likely my freedom. Definitely any hope for a future that doesn't involve the hiring fairs.

I want this *over with*.

Ricochet rubs his chin against me. He's trying to cheer me up. He has no idea that soon we'll never see each other again.

I run my hand down his velvety nose. Just being together a little while longer.

Something tugs at my arm. I open my eyes and squint because a stream of sunlight is pouring through the trees and into my face. The tug happens again. It's Ricochet, who's cropped all the grass and stems within the lead rope's reach and now he's trying to get to a juicy patch just beyond.

I'm wide awake now. It's midmorning, and I've been lying here long past the time I could sidle up to the guards at the city gate and turn myself in quietly.

Cursing, I scramble to my feet and take stock. I don't remember pulling the saddle off Ricochet last night, or fashioning his reins into a lead rope so I could take the bit out of his mouth. I check the leather message bag I must have used as a pillow—if the aching grooves in my face are any proof—but sure enough, it's completely empty. Not even a copper caught in the seams.

No reason to hurry now. It's going to be very public.

By daylight, the greenwood is transformed. It's almost like being on a trail ride. Leaves and fronds sparkle with dew and there's birdsong, lots of it, as if today isn't the worst day of my life.

Ricochet is scruffy, covered in mud and dried sweat, with thistles and leaves and burrs stuck in his mane and tail. Even his white stockings are gone, caked with grime well past his knees.

"Torsten will give you a bath," I tell him cheerfully, because I might have to say goodbye, but at least our last moments together can be happy. "You're filthy, and you smell. Then again, so do I. Sorry I have to put this saddle on you. It's too heavy for me to carry. I know you're tired. But it won't be long now."

It takes a lot to keep smiling. It's easier if I don't talk, so I pull all the burrs and thistles out of Ricochet's mane and tail, finger-combing both slow and careful. Pulling apart knots instead of forcing them. Smiling. Hard.

Finally there's nothing left to do. I *clickclick* to Ricochet and lead him through the verge, out of the greenwood and onto the tidy carriageway. The city walls get broader and higher with every step. Beyond the cheerful market crowds, I can see the usual two guards in full livery. Their flintlock muskets. Their swords.

"I love you, Ricochet," I whisper, "even if you'll never be mine."

I can do this. He'll be safe. So will the others. They are not just outrider horses. They are *horses.*

"Hey. Hey!" A narrow-faced string bean of a man grabs at the halter of a chestnut gelding with a white star and two white socks that a constable is leading away. "This horse is mine! I never stole him. He's been in the sale pen for nearly a fortnight. Ask anyone here!"

I want no part of constables. They work for the city and not the king, so I detour Ricochet till he's mostly hidden behind a manure cart.

"I've never been anywhere near the racetrack!" the string-bean man goes on, loud and insulted. "And do I look like a half-grown girl? When you find that kid, I hope you hang her for the trouble she's causing everyone here! Bad enough no one's allowed to buy or sell any horses till you find that one of the king's, but why does the whole market have to be hassled? You gonna impound every chestnut horse with any white on him?"

My whole stomach turns to ice. Very quietly I tug

Ricochet into motion and lead him back the way we came. There's a wall of constables between here and the city gate, and there'll be another set of them on guard there. Maybe more.

There's no way any of them will get Master Harold. If I turn up with Ricochet, I'm going straight to the gatehouse, and from there to the gallows. It won't matter who speaks for me.

As far as the king is concerned, I'm a horse thief.

16

HORSE THIEVES ARE hanged. I'm done for.

We hurry through the greenwood. I'm stumbling every other step. The reins are sweaty in my hands. Ricochet behind me clops along like all this is ordinary.

Deirdre will have rushed straight to the track stablemaster with a breathless, panicky story. *She's always had her eye on that horse. Never let anyone else ride him. She was just waiting for the moment our backs were turned.*

By tomorrow, both Mother and Father will find their hiring fair contracts canceled. Bad conduct, they'll be told. A violation of the morality clause that allows for instant termination if something they do reflects badly on the dignity of their employer.

Torsten, too. He's likely gone already.

My toe catches a rock and I pitch forward, nearly dropping my empty message bag. It won't matter that I didn't steal Ricochet. One of the king's jockeys said I did, and there's no reason for anyone to doubt her word.

Greta will be arrested on the common. The ponies will be sold. The little house on Edge Lane was never ours to start with, so the landlord will reclaim it and keep whatever my family is forced to leave behind.

The bench. The stone fireplace that Father put in himself.

My wooden toy horses.

The constables will shove and hassle my family through the lanes, then the streets, all the way to the city gates. Then the brutes will brand each of them on the hand with whatever hot metal is lying around.

Even if I leave Ricochet somewhere safe and turn myself in, no one will believe a word about the Night Ride. Not the guardsmen or constables. Not the magistrates. Definitely not the king. It'll look like I'm blathering anything that has the smallest chance of saving my neck.

Ricochet and I can't stay out here forever. The king will send his rangers to arrest the thief, and I have no idea how to survive in the greenwood. Ricochet will be okay for a while eating only grass, but he has to eat constantly, and he can't do that if we're hiding.

The sunlight goes blinding. We've stumbled into a meadow. There's a creek, and Ricochet pulls me toward it. When he steps in to drink, the mud washes from his fetlocks and the white beneath emerges.

The constables must not have stopped us because his

legs were filthy. No white markings to draw their eye.

I can't help but laugh.

The meadow reminds me of the one on the Night Ride trail. Packed with every kind of wildflower and loud with birdsong and circled by thick, imposing trees.

Somewhere to rest. To take a breath.

I unbuckle Ricochet's saddle and take off his bridle. I don't like doing it—if he spooks and runs, it'll take forever to catch him—but he didn't run away last night, and we both need a break.

Then I pull off my boots and socks, and dip my feet in the stream. It feels so freeing and glorious that I wriggle my toes and splash-kick a few times just to watch the droplets glitter. Ricochet has moved on to nibbling at the long grasses on the stream bank, and all he does is flick his tail.

I tip backward into the crunchy, flowery grass. The ground warm beneath me, my face to the sun. A girl out with her horse on a beautiful summer morning. The way I always pictured it.

The way it almost was, but never will be.

The meadow is full of horse sounds. Ricochet's sounds. *Shuffrustle.* Long legs in tall grass. *Thudkritch.* Hooves on dirt. And over all of it, the long, musical rumble of the creek.

When I sit up, Ricochet is peaceably browsing, but his saddle is gone. I scrabble to my feet, scanning wildly. A small smudge of motion at the other end of the meadow is *shuffrustling* and *thudkritching* the saddle toward the greenwood.

It's a little kid!

"Hey!" I shout. "That's not yours!"

I dart a glance at Ricochet, but he's still grazing, so I take off after the kid. I expect him to drop the saddle and run, but he puts his head down and *shuffrustles* faster. He's maybe five, so I catch him easily, but when I try to take the saddle, he winds his body around it and goes limp, sinking to the ground.

"What are you doing?" I almost laugh until it occurs to me that he's a distraction. His father or brother is likely leading away Ricochet right now.

Only Ricochet is rolling, his legs kicking gleefully as he twists and swivels.

"Stealing this." The boy says it like I have mud for brains. He looks up at me through a wild tangle of curly yellow hair.

"Well. You can't." I kneel so we're at eye level. "I still need it."

"I need it more. Already stole a horse. Now I need a saddle so I can ride with the cadre."

"Cadre?" I echo. "Are you a bandit?"

"Trying to be." He's sullen, like he can't believe his clever plan fell through and he got caught.

It's a long shot, but I hope hard and ask, "Do you know a boy named Paolo?"

"Maybe," the kid replies warily.

"Can you take me to him?"

When the kid's eyes narrow, I wince and hurry on, "I mean, *if* you knew a boy named Paolo, would you ask him to meet me here? We're friends. You can tell him it's Sonnia. From the racetrack."

The boy looks down at the saddle. "If I do that, will you let me steal this?"

"Then it wouldn't really be stealing, would it? It would be like I was giving it to you, and you have to steal it for it to count. Right?"

I'm only guessing here, but the kid's face falls like melting ice cream. "Yeah."

He lets go of the saddle and it topples at my feet. He scowls, glum and uncooperative, and if there's one thing a younger sister teaches you, it's how to get little kids on your side. And why it's usually a good idea.

As I lean to pick the saddle up, I shift so my empty message bag slides off my arm and into the grass. I heft the saddle as if the bag doesn't exist, and the boy is trying very hard not to look at it, quivering like a puppy when you're getting its supper ready.

"I'm going to see what my horse is doing," I tell him. "Don't worry. You look like you're good at stealing. There's bound to be something nearby."

His little hands are darting even before my back is turned.

All afternoon I sit against a tree, watching Ricochet graze and reminding myself that when Deirdre had nowhere else to go, Paolo's family took her in. Surely they'll do the same for me and Ricochet. Even for a few days.

If the kid really does know Paolo. If the joy of stealing something doesn't make him forget to relay my message.

If the king's rangers don't find me first.

Daylight is fading when Paolo appears at the far edge of the meadow. He waves as he comes near, making sure both Ricochet and I see him.

I will never have a better friend.

His arms are full of things. There's a tether pin and a big coil of rope for Ricochet, to keep him from wandering off. There's a thick wool blanket for me and a waterskin full of cider, and best of all, a huge basket of meat and bread and cheese.

My smile fades. I wouldn't need any of this gear if Paolo had come to bring us to the bandit camp. Without a word, I shove the tether pin into the ground, call Ricochet with our whistle, and tie the rope to his halter.

"Look." Paolo sighs. "It's just that Deirdre is in the middle of this, and she'll be mad and scared and she knows how to find us. There'll be rangers. Constables, too. My mother says we can't take the risk. It's not fair, and I said so, but . . . I'm sorry."

I pull in a deep breath, let it out slow. "No need to be sorry. It's not your fault."

He shrugs like he doesn't agree, and after a moment

he reaches into the basket, splits a roll, puts some meat and cheese on it, and offers it to me.

It should bother me that this food was stolen, but I sink onto the ground next to him and take the sandwich.

"I wish I knew what to do next," I whisper. "I thought I did, but now I'm afraid to do anything. All this happened because I was only thinking about myself. What was good for me and what I wanted."

Paolo frowns. "If that was true, you'd still be doing the Night Ride and packing dinars into your purse. If you mean to put a stop to it, you're not thinking about yourself. You're thinking about the outrider horses."

"But I did the Night Ride for all those weeks, even knowing it was dangerous, because it was the only way to get what I wanted."

"Well. Maybe." Paolo picks a grass stem and splits it with a thumbnail. "But then you changed your mind."

"After Hollyhock got *hurt*! He would have been someone's supper if you hadn't been there to save him!"

"It can take a lot for someone to change their mind," Paolo replies. "We're used to seeing the world one way. It makes sense. It makes our lives easier. The hard part is when you learn something that disrupts your idea of how the world is. Then you have a choice—keep thinking what you've always thought, even though it doesn't feel as right or certain anymore. Or change your mind."

Evening is drifting in. The greenwood that hugs the meadow is turning rich shades of dark, and a bright sweep of stars is prickling into being. Ricochet has arranged himself into a hollow near the tree line. He looks so cozy that I almost want to tuck him in with the blanket Paolo brought.

"A lot of people never change their minds," Paolo adds quietly. "It's comforting, thinking you have all the answers. If you think it, it must be right, and anyone who doesn't agree is not only wrong but an utter fool. If you're the one to change your mind, you must have been wrong. And that makes *you* the fool."

It feels like all I've done lately is change my mind, but I don't feel like a fool for doing it. Mostly I feel a little sick that I spent so much time convincing myself that having happy memories of someone makes them a good person.

Later, once Paolo has left for the bandit camp and the black sky glitters with stars, I lie down near Ricochet so our heads are inches apart. His breathing is smooth and even, his rest peaceful, and in this moment he is my horse.

The rangers are coming. The bandits can't help me. It's only a matter of time now.

I'm going to be caught. They're going to take Ricochet. The best I can hope for is that the king won't be able to stomach hanging a girl the same age as his daughters, and I'll be branded and banished along with my family. What I should do now is plan what to say to the king to save my neck.

What do you plan to do?

The way she said it. As if big and unimaginable things were within my power.

Because they are. I can put a stop to the Night Ride. I can save *all* the outrider horses.

The whole city is convinced I'm a horse thief. Deirdre and the track stablemaster have made sure of that, and the king won't believe a word that comes out of my mouth. Not unless there's proof.

I lie on my back in the meadow as the stars grow thicker. Next time the moon is up, I will give him proof.

I spend the days saying goodbye to Ricochet. Petting him. Whispering into his mane. Telling him how much I love him. How much I'm going to miss him.

But the night finally comes, and by the time darkness has settled and the moon has risen, fat and glowing, I've saddled him and given him a handkerchief full of blackberries from Paolo's basket. I've cried all I'm going to cry, and I'm ready for this to be over.

Now we're waiting in the carriageway that leads to the city gate. The moon is finally in the right place over the horizon, and I've made enough racket that we'll be easy to find in this big wash of silver light.

Ricochet is whuffling, dancing in place. Every muscle is quivering. He knows what we do when we saddle up at night.

We ride to win.

"You there. You with the horse." A man's voice. Deep, like it comes from the bottom of a barrel. "Stay where you are and be ready to give an account of yourself to the king's rangers."

They emerge as shadows from the greenwood, and a twinge of alarm runs through me. Rangers have the same training as fleet riders. Their horses, too. They know how to pursue a suspect through the worst terrain.

They might catch me before we get anywhere near the pasture behind the racetrack.

"I believe you're looking for a horse thief." My voice is stronger than I feel, and sassier. "Girl, half grown? Chestnut gelding with four white stockings and a blaze down his nose?"

I turn Ricochet so the rangers can get a good look.

"Honey, this is no joke," one says sternly. "If you get down now, maybe—"

I *clickclick* to Ricochet and press him with my calves and away he goes, flying through the moonlit greenwood like he was born doing it. The rangers shout in a wordless clamor and hooves pound behind us, but I don't look back.

There's no trail. Just thick, ancient trees. I whisper a prayer and hold on.

We're going too fast. We'll get to the pasture before anyone else on the Night Ride, and the jockeys and spectators can just scatter into the darkness like they were never there, and all of this will be for nothing.

I can't slow down, though.

The sound of Ricochet's hooves changes from the dull, damp thudding of the greenwood to something sharper, more hollow and echoing. We're on a trail. We're getting close to the track, but the rangers are gaining on us.

Ricochet banks a hard left and the back pasture fence comes into view, jarring frantically with his pace. Beyond I can see shadows in the ring, some horse-shaped and others human, and farther distant are the pay table and its crowd of excited trainers and grooms and horseboys. The gate is standing open, and someone is galloping through.

Astrid, I think. She was so sure I wouldn't ruin the Ride. Some part of her thought one day I'd come around. That I could be one of them.

Ricochet sails over the fence, clean and graceful the way he always does, and when I sneak a look behind me, the rangers are piling through the gate. There are six of them. They wear the king's livery, and they are armed.

I steer Ricochet toward the chalk line and Benno, but as we near, I realize he's not alone. Deirdre is there, along with a handful of jockeys and trainers, and they're telling her she needs to calm down. The Ride is going fine. She's overreacting. No need to disrupt the pay table because of some girl and a worthless outrider horse.

I rein in the *worthless outrider horse* so the rangers are

all in a cluster behind me, but instead of riding him in a cooldown lap around the fence, I pull a tight circle and slide off in front of Deirdre. The rangers are close behind me, and I flinch away from the creak of leather and the swish of boots in grass.

The jingle of handcuffs.

"Flags?" Deirdre must not recognize me, because she holds out her hand like I'm any other rider.

That's when the shouting starts. That's when shadows try and fail to scatter every which way.

I throw my arms around Ricochet's neck for one last hug. He's still breathing hard, and I tell him I'm sorry.

Then I hold out my wrists, and a ranger slams down the silver cuffs.

17

ON MY FIRST day in the gatehouse, I'm put in a cell in the topmost tower with a privy bucket, a loaf of bread, and a jug of water. I spend the day on tiptoe at the tiny window, trying to work out whether carpenters have started on the gallows.

On the second day, magistrates arrive to question me. Three of them, one by one, then two sergeants-at-law, and a trailing line of royal officials with more titles than I thought could exist. They all ask the same thing, and it isn't *why did you steal Ricochet?*

It's *what do you know about this illegal horse race?*

I will always love the Deirdre who brought a whirl of fun and happiness into my childhood, but I tell the magistrates everything about the junior racing cadre and their hopes for the future, where those kids came from and why, how the Night Ride was both a carrot and a stick, what happened to Hollyhock.

Pay table, they scribble. *Illegal gambling. No share granted to the king.*

"I know you probably arrested the kids in the junior racing cadre," I say, "but it's not their fault."

"We arrested *everyone*," a constable says sternly from his sentry post at the door, but the magistrate looks up from the heavy sheet of paper in front of him. He's well-fed like everyone from townhouses, but he has a kind face and wears woolen clothing instead of heavy brocade robes and piles of gold jewelry.

"They were coerced, then? With threats? Violence?" The magistrate sounds genuinely concerned. "Forced to engage in this race? *You* were coerced?"

I look down. It doesn't take either one of those when you're a lane kid. We all chose to ride. Even me.

If you can call it a choice.

Before he leaves, the magistrate says I can send a message to my parents if I want to. I'm so relieved that they haven't yet been exiled that I babble some nonsense about how much I love them and miss them and to hug the ponies and Greta for me.

It's only when he's gone that I realize I should have asked them to visit. Bring my wooden toy horses, in case these walls are the last thing I ever see.

On the third day I'm drawing Ricochet in the dust when an official scrapes open the door and jerks his chin at the corridor beyond.

This must be it. Time to hear my sentence.

I follow without a word. My heart is hammering so big and throbby that I sway on my feet. The official leads me through dim passageways that change from stone to rough wood to smooth, shiny planks, until there's carpet under my feet and paintings of horses on the walls and a huge fireplace and big windows that spill huge panels of light onto—

The king.

I'd know him anywhere. Everyone in Mael Dunn knows him. He and his family ride in processions through town during all the holiday parades. His daughters wear cloaks with fur collars and throw candy and toys and coppers from silken bags for children to gather. He rides a huge white stallion named Polydorus, and he gave Torsten a job that has probably already been taken away.

The official elbows me, and I curtsy even though I haven't worn a dress in months. I don't think my old school dress even fits me anymore. But that won't matter. School is the last of my worries now.

The last of Greta's, too. There'll be no place in a schoolroom in this realm or any other for someone with a branded hand.

The king gestures to a stool on one side of a sprawling table. It's stationed across from his oversized plush settee beneath the floor-to-ceiling windows. Somehow I manage to cross the thick red carpet and fall onto the hard wooden seat.

"Well, then." The king's voice is measured as he

strokes his dark moustache. "You're the girl who stole one of my horses."

"Ricochet." I sit up straighter. "His name is Ricochet, and is he all right? Someone took him away after we broke up the Ride. Is he back with Master Harold? In his old stall?"

The king frowns the smallest bit. "Yes. He's at the royal stables and perfectly sound."

I let out a long, trembling breath and blink away tears. Given everyone who's going to suffer because of what I did, at least Ricochet won't be one of them.

"Most people who get a clemency hearing use it to beg for their lives." The king leans forward. "Not ask about the well-being of someone else's horse."

If I were Greta, I'd know what *clemency* means, but it seems like the king is either looking for a reason not to hang me, or a reason he should.

I've repeated the same story to magistrates and sergeants-at-law and royal officials for two whole days. If the king hasn't already decided what's to become of me, I doubt there's anything I can say now to change his mind.

So I lift my chin and say, "I didn't steal Ricochet."

The king's brows go up, and my belly plummets down and down. It's hard not to think of a horse as your own when you take care of him every day and you know his favorite treats and where he likes to be scratched. You can't steal something that's already yours.

But Ricochet isn't mine. He was never going to be, even when I was saving up my pony ride coppers with more hope than sense.

"All right, yes, I did take Ricochet from the racetrack without permission." My belly churns. "I'd have brought all the outriders with me if I could. But everyone knows how much I love him, and I wasn't going to take the chance that someone would hurt him to teach me a lesson."

The king's face is red, like he's trying not to lose his temper.

"I was always going to give Ricochet back," I whisper. "I just . . . I knew I would lose him for good once I did."

"No need to worry about the horses at the track anymore," the king growls. "Right now they're being cared for by men from the royal stables whom I trust personally. Racehorses, workhorses, outriders, all of them. Every last person who had anything to do with my racetrack is now out of a job—and being interrogated."

I breathe out, long and relieved, but now that it's done, it feels like something adults should have taken care of long ago, so there's be no shadow of the gallows over me.

"You disagree?" The king peers at me.

"No. Sire." I squirm on the hard seat. "Only sad for my friends. The kids in the junior racing cadre. Worried for them, too."

"The magistrates have already questioned the boys—and girl—in Deirdre's so-called junior racing cadre. There's nothing to be gained in punishing them, and they've already been released."

Released. Surely. Back to the lanes and hiring fairs.

"I don't think much of the *girl jockey*," the king goes on, like even the words taste bad, "but I admit I like the idea of boys being formally taught the right way to ride a racehorse. How to understand a horse and work with him in partnership. So I'll be establishing a royal racing academy, with retired jockeys as instructors. No one who might have a conflict of interest."

"Does that mean . . . can my friends be in it?"

"They will be allowed to try out." The king says it like he's giving them a gift. Like they should take it and be grateful.

It's more than I expected. Way more than I hoped for. My friends will have the chance that Deirdre promised them—a way to escape the lanes and the hiring fairs. They can build the junior racing cadre they always should have had.

"Astrid, too?" It's not like the king can hang me twice. "You said boys, but she's a good rider, and she cares about horses."

"I don't know." He sighs harshly. "After Deirdre, it's going to be hard enough feeling that I can trust anyone at the racetrack. Everyone knew what was going on with the Night Ride. Even the *horseboys* knew!" The king slams a fist on the armrest. "Yet no one so much as breathed a word to me."

I nod and study my feet. No need to tell him why. He already knows.

"No one but you," he adds. "If you hadn't done what you did, the Night Ride would still be happening. I'd have no idea what the girl jockey was getting away with. What that scoundrel of a track stablemaster was overlooking, how much he was profiting."

"Wh-what will happen to her?" I ask.

"Exile. With the brand."

I'm glad I'm sitting down. There's horse harm, then there's horse thievery.

"All right. I'm guilty." I twist my shirttail in my lap. "I took Ricochet. I did it knowing what would happen if I got caught, but he's not in danger anymore. I know you love all your horses. If he were mine and I didn't know where he was and I thought someone stole him, I'd punish them too. Only please don't punish my family. They had nothing to do with this."

"I have no intention of punishing your family," the king replies, "and I definitely have no intention of punishing you."

My eyes come up. I blink hard.

"I don't like being made a fool. You're the one who opened my eyes to it." He shakes his head. "I still can't believe all of it went on under my nose!"

The king keeps talking. How Master Harold will be

in charge at the racetrack for a while. How racehorses, outriders, and workhorses will all be safe and cared for, and everyone hired will be accountable to the king personally. How he's already dropped the track's minimum bets since they kept coming up in a lot of confessions.

I'm still stuck on *no intention* and *punishing*.

"Ah." I remember how to breathe. "So I'm not to be hanged?"

The king laughs. "I should think not! Besides, the horse was returned. Consider all charges dropped."

This morning I woke up in a cell in the gatehouse and spent most of the day with one eye on the common just in case the carpenters arrived. Tonight I'll be at home. I'll sleep in my own bed. Tomorrow I'll be—

Back to pony rides. School. The hiring fairs.

"For someone who just received a royal pardon," says the king, "you don't look happy."

"No, thank you, I really am grateful." I try to smile, but now that I have my life, all I can think of is the future I'm looking toward.

Which is no future at all.

The king smiles again, bigger this time, and replies, "My daughters are your age. I can wait forever."

"I just . . . gave up a lot. Now I have nothing."

"Don't you plan to apply to the royal racing academy?"

I shrug. It's hard to imagine returning to the track. Even knowing Deirdre won't be there. The other kids all know what I did. What I took away from them. Besides, the idea of endless post parades and constant competition makes me shudder.

"Well, what *do* you want?" the king asks.

"Ricochet." It's foolish and big and unimaginable, but I don't hesitate. "He's the reason I went to the track stable in the first place. I started doing the Night Ride to keep him safe, but when I began earning all that money, I figured it would be the only chance I'd have to save up enough to buy him. I've only ever wanted him to be my own horse."

Only Ricochet is not a want. He never has been, because if he's a want, he's a thing. I want things *for* him, the way I want them for my brother and my sister and my parents and my friends.

Ricochet may be the only friend I have left.

"Here's the twenty-two coppers I saved before I knew he cost five *thousand*." I pull the scruffy bag of coins from my jacket's inner pocket and empty them onto the table. "I know I can't afford him, and besides, he's yours, and also I have no way to keep him now that the Ride is broken up, so I guess it's best he stays where he is."

"Hmm." The king leans forward in his plush chair. "Then would you agree to be a fleet rider? That way you could ride Ricochet all the time."

"Don't you have to be fifteen and, well, get a royal invitation?"

"I think I can arrange a royal invitation."

I smile in spite of myself, and the king goes on, "From what I've learned of the Night Ride, you already have better training than most new fleet riders. And I can be sure you'll never run your horse too hard or take chances with his safety just to get a message through."

Hours in the saddle. Days sometimes. Endless trail rides, just me and Ricochet.

"It'll be short runs to start with, until the fleet master approves longer missions. Shares are paid on quarter days, but you'll get a bonus of five dinars right away so you can outfit yourself properly."

Shares. A fleet rider gets three shares of everything the horses earn. That's coppers to send home. Coppers to save.

"Well?" The king lifts his brows. "Do you want the position or not?"

I'm on my feet. I'm halfway around the table before I remember that this is the anointed sovereign of Mael Dunn and not someone I should hug. Instead I stand before him, knotting and unknotting my hands, and I whisper *thank you* again and again until he calls for someone to escort me home.

It's been three days since I was released from the gatehouse, and this morning I'm expected at the royal stables for my first day as a fleet rider.

I barely sleep. I'm wide awake when the sky is still dark, but I don't need much light to put on my fancy riding clothes. Mother took them to the sweatshop and sneaked them into a vat of mysterious liquids, and they're perfect again. I bought a second shirt and breeches with my bonus, along with a good helmet, all of it waiting in a rucksack by the front door.

Father has already left on his deliveries, but Greta is sitting at the table with a steaming mug in front of her. She's wearing a green dress that's only a little frayed at the cuffs, and there's a copybook at her elbow.

When I got home, we hugged and she said she was glad I was safe. I told her I was sorry for making her do all the pony rides, and she accepted my apology.

She didn't ask any Greta questions, though—what went on during a typical day at the racetrack, how odds were figured, how many people came to the races, what the other stablehands were like. She didn't even ask about the Night Ride, and now she doesn't look away from her tea when I dish up a bowl of porridge and sit across from her.

The house is so quiet that I can hear the ponies out back chewing hay. I squirm and say, "You must be excited to be back at school."

"Mother told me I had to thank you for using some of your bonus to pay for it. So thank you."

Greta says it to her mug, her voice flat as paper.

"Are you ever going to stop being mad at me?" I whisper.

"I'm not angry with you, Sonnia. I'm just . . . Torsten's

in royal service. You're in royal service. Me?" She coughs a bitter laugh. "Might as well go to the hiring fairs right now and save you some coppers."

"But you're in school again. You love school!"

"For half days. So what? It's not like anything's going to come of it."

"Only until I get my first shares," I protest. "Then you can go all day! Master Harold will let us keep the ponies in the pasture with the retired fleet horses and we can visit them."

"Half day, full day—it doesn't matter." Greta sighs. "Even before I had to quit, Mistress Crumb was already saying there wasn't much left she could teach me. I'd have to go to the academy for townhouse girls, and it won't just be a matter of money there."

I stir my porridge. It's thin and bland, nothing like the stuff from the track cookhouse, packed with raisins and swimming with molasses.

"I'm sorry I said anything," Greta mutters. "It's foolish. I can't go to the academy. Simple as that."

"You get to want things," I reply, gripping my spoon. "You get to want anything."

"No, I don't." She looks me in the eye. "You do."

I stare hard into my breakfast. Behind us is my rucksack by the door, packed and ready for my new life as a fleet rider for the king of Mael Dunn.

The only way kids like us—girls like us—get anything better is when we make it happen for ourselves.

Only Deirdre didn't mean *ourselves*. She meant herself, and I was to do the same if I could, however I could.

No matter who got stepped on.

I take a deep breath. "If you can pass the entrance exam and bluff through the interview and get Mistress Crumb to give you a recommendation, I'll pay your way through the academy."

Greta peers at me warily. "It wouldn't be cheap. Beyond the fees, I'd also need books. Decent clothes. An astrolabe. What about Ricochet?"

"Oh, I still plan to buy him one day. It'll just take a little longer." I smile to show I mean it even as my stomach flips and flips again. "Fortunately, he's the patient type."

"Going to the academy would be amazing," Greta whispers, "but I don't know that I can do all those things."

"I'm not saying you have to, or even that you should. But if you *want* to, I will help you make it happen." Quietly I add, "I love Ricochet, but you're my sister."

Greta runs a finger around the rim of her mug. She murmurs something that might be *thank you*.

The sky is getting light. I'm expected at the royal stables before the first chime from the clock tower. I finish my porridge in heaping bites, and I'm shouldering my rucksack when Greta says, "Be safe out there, all right? If there's any counting to be done, let Ricochet handle it."

I laugh aloud, then stick my tongue out at her. She does the same, and then I smile for real because this is Greta truly accepting my apology.

The royal stables are just how I remember them: warm, gently lit with safety lamps, and already bustling despite the hour. The gather point for fleet riders is at the far end of the corridor, but it seems like I'm the first one here. I'm about to take a seat on a bale of straw when Master Harold turns up. He's leading Ricochet by the halter, and he's carrying a red bridle.

"Good news. The king has agreed to your price and accepted your offer." Master Harold drops the loops of leather into my hands.

It takes a moment. The red bridle. Ricochet nudging my elbow for the carrot he knows is in my pocket.

"M-my price?" I stammer.

"Apparently during your conversation with the king the other day, you offered twenty-two coppers for the chestnut fleet horse known as Ricochet, and the king feels that amount is acceptable." Master Harold smiles. "Ricochet is your horse now. The red bridle has his name on it, see? His and yours."

My mouth is open. Words are coming out, but none make sense. "But he . . . I can't afford . . . the stable . . ."

"If you want to keep him anywhere else, you'll have to pay boarding." Master Harold looks very pleased with himself. "Fleet horses who live in the royal stable have their keep paid for by the king."

I drop the red bridle on the bale of straw and hug Master Harold. No curtsying. Just a hug for a man who's got so much goodness in his heart that he will always help where he can, wherever he can.

"What are you waiting for?" Master Harold pulls away and tries to be the gruff taskmaster I always mistook him for. "The fleet captain will be here any moment and that horse of yours isn't anywhere near ready."

That horse of yours.

Ricochet noses me again and whuffles. I grin and give him the carrot. Then I head over to the tack shed to get the distance saddle that all the fleet horses wear.

I have a good long ride ahead of me.